Salvation

Blue Moon Saloon
Book 4

by Anna Lowe

Twin Moon Press

Editing by Lisa A. Hollett

Covert art by Jacqueline Sweet

Contents

Other books in this series

Blue Moon Saloon

Perfection (a short story prequel)

Damnation (Book 1)

Temptation (Book 2)

Redemption (Book 3)

Salvation (Book 4)

Deception (Book 5)

Celebration (a holiday treat)

visit www.annalowebooks.com

Free Books

Get your free e-books now!

Sign up for my newsletter at *annalowebooks.com* to get three free books!

- *Desert Wolf*: Friend or Foe (Book 1.1 in the Twin Moon Ranch series)

- *Off the Charts* (the prequel to the Serendipity Adventure series)

- *Perfection* (the prequel to the Blue Moon Saloon series)

Prologue

Clouds drifted silently across the midnight sky, obscuring the full moon. The pines were still as the bear lumbered beneath them, favoring his right leg. He paused to sniff the air. It was dry — painfully dry — and carried a thousand unfamiliar scents. The fragrance of hardy wildflowers danced in the high-altitude desert air. The fresh scent of ponderosa and sycamore lay beneath the rest like a carpet, and behind it all was a whiff of burned-out brush fire that made his hackles rise.

It was a warm night — warm, silent, and somehow foreboding, given the way the shadows mimicked his every move.

Where are you going? they seemed to taunt him. *Why?*

Damned if he knew. He was many hungry months and hundreds of miles away from the ashes of home. Tired, too. Bone-tired. Yet the stars kept pulling him onward, whispering into his mind.

You're nearly there. Nearly there.

Nearly where?

Early on in his long march south, he had roared the question into the night. Now, he just chuffed and walked on, wondering how much of his mind he'd lost from remaining in bear form for too long. Of course, staying human was just as dangerous; every shifter needed to satisfy both sides of his soul. But Todd wasn't sure what was left of his soul. He'd never felt emptier or more alone.

Nearly there, the stars promised.

Were the stars playing games with him or leading him to salvation? The spirits of his ancestors congregated around Ursa Major, the Great Bear, and they twinkled at him from between the interlocking pine boughs. They wouldn't lie, would they?

1

He'd been wandering for more nights than he could count, swinging his head left and right to check his surroundings. That was a new habit he'd developed since the hearing had been pounded out of him in an attack that had nearly cost him his life. Sometimes, he'd whip his head around, imagining the snap of a twig or the hoot of an owl, but most of the time, his ears registered nothing but a quiet buzz.

He swiped an angry paw at his left ear. If only he could chase away the sound the way he could shoo away a bee. It was growing worse now — a clanging ring that wouldn't stop, as if he'd lingered too long and too close to the noontime call of church bells and had gone deaf from that, instead of from the beating of bats and bricks.

He gritted his teeth, fighting the memories away. He would have been better off dying as he'd been destined to. Death would have been fine because he had fought for a worthy cause. For duty, for honor, for love. What more could a bear desire?

But instead of fading away and reaching for the light that had called to him from heaven, he'd been fool enough to listen to a voice that had pulled him back from the edge.

Stay with me. Don't die. Not now. Not like this.

If it hadn't been the sweetest, fairest voice he'd ever heard, he might have ignored it and moved on to join his ancestors among the stars.

Think of mountain meadows in spring, the kind, feminine voice had pleaded. *Think of a clear, cool summer creek. Think of berries growing thick in the fall.*

And damn it, he'd pictured one beautiful season after another and gotten greedy for life all over again.

Just think of all the things you'll live to enjoy again. Stay with me...

The speaker had tricked him, because she'd left out a few important things. Like the crushing guilt of surviving a night most of his clanmates had fallen victim to. The heavy silence in his ears, the gnawing ache in his leg. The feeling of being alone. Why live life as a wreck of a bear or a wreck of a man?

He stopped and shook his fur so hard his teeth rattled then walked slowly onward. Maybe if he found whatever it was that pulled him like a magnet, he could find peace again.

The buzz in his ears rose and fell. It warbled and varied in pitch like. . . like a sonorous wolf howl. That much, he could tell — more from tiny movements in the air than actual sound. The fur on the centerline of his back stood up as he halted in his tracks and eyed a ridge to the north. Wolves?

There were good wolves and bad wolves, and not even a big, bad grizzly was safe from a pack of the latter, as he'd learned the hard way one fateful night. A night he'd laid it all on the line to protect his cousin's mate as he'd promised to. He would do it all over again, too, because bears knew all about duty and honor and respect for the power of love. Even knowing he would come out of it damaged in more ways than one, he'd do it all over again. He had no regrets.

Except one. One terrible regret from the time before the attack. Something that tainted his honor and haunted his soul.

He sniffed until he spotted the wolves howling on the ridge. Two of them, sitting side by side, their noses pointed at the moon.

Why wolves howled, he had no clue, but he'd never been more tempted to try it than in the bleakness of the past few months.

Then they broke off — he could tell when the ringing in his ears went monotone again — and snapped their muzzles in his direction. A moment later, they came stalking down the slope, right at him.

He watched and waited, sniffing the air as they loped up and circled him. They kept their noses high and their shoulders low, ready to flee. The dark-haired she-wolf circled him clockwise while the gold-hued male paced the other way, growling quietly the whole time. He could tell from the angle of the wolves' jaws, from the tingle in his ears. He let a warning rumble build in his own throat in reply.

Shifters. Werewolves. Every nerve in his body went on high alert.

Each time the wolves' paths crossed, they brushed along against each other in long, deliberate strokes that showed them to be lovers. Mates.

3

Todd growled low and long in warning. He had no desire to make trouble for a pair of destined mates. Let them live and love and be happy. Him, he was just passing through.

The she-wolf stopped suddenly and cocked her head, staring deep into his eyes with a startled look. Her jaw fell open, and a whisper tickled the edge of his mind.

Todd?

He backed up a step. How did she know his name? Who was she? How could her thoughts reach into his mind? Only closely related shifters or packmates could do that, and she was a stranger.

Or was she?

The she-wolf's gaze went from quizzical to joyous to mournful, all in the blink of an eye. As if she knew some terrible secret he was about to find out the hard way.

Todd, is it really you?

How to answer that? He wasn't the same man — or bear — he used to be.

It's me, she said. *Janna.*

Before he could make any attempt at an answer, though, the wolves glanced left, just as a new scent reached his nose. He whipped around.

Bear, the musky scent told him.

Big bear, a heavy step vibrating through the ground said.

Alpha bear, the animal's tall, confident stance announced the second Todd spotted it stalking toward him. Every step the grizzly took claimed possession of the land, the air, the mountainside.

This is all mine, the alpha's countenance said. *How dare you enter my turf?*

The wolves ran over and flanked the grizzly like a couple of sentries at their king's side. Todd stood still, holding his breath. Why did the bear seem familiar? Why was his heart leaping in relief instead of pounding in preparation for a brawl?

The alpha bear took two steps forward and reared up on his back legs, casting a shadow over Todd. He showed his teeth, tilted his head, and finally chuffed.

Todd's mind spun. He knew that sandy brown bear. He knew those brilliant blue eyes.

The air around the grizzly blurred as the beast became a man — a man who came out of his shift without so much as a shiver and fixed him straight in the eye. Slowly, the man dropped to a crouch and came eye to eye. His lips moved, and even if Todd could hear, he would have missed the words. His mind was too busy processing a thousand impossible thoughts.

Soren? His cousin, Soren?

Todd? Soren's voice boomed into his mind.

It was the clearest, loudest sound he'd heard in a long, long time, even if it didn't pass through his ears first.

Soren?

Soren nodded warily. *Jesus, man. Is it really you?*

Todd nodded slowly, carefully. Soren was his best friend. His cousin. The heir to the alpha position in their home clan — a clan that had been decimated months ago.

It really was him. Soren, whom Todd had served loyally except for one bitter betrayal he would never forgive himself for. Soren would never forgive him either, once he found out.

What about Sarah? Todd managed. Damn, even though he was shooting thoughts into his cousin's mind, his voice was still shaky.

Soren nodded slowly. *She's here. She survived, thanks to you. She's my mate.*

A thousand emotions hit Todd like a volley of arrows out of the blue. Relief. Wonder. Happiness for his cousin. But steamrolling all that aside was shame — the deepest, most piercing arrow of them all, striking him in the corner of his heart.

It took everything he had to keep his eyes level with Soren's instead of dropping to the ground. He had to be honest and admit what had happened between him and Sarah a year ago. A night when he'd been overcome by some crazy impulse and betrayed his cousin by sleeping with his mate.

Soren took a deep breath exactly when Todd did, and they both sent the same thought to each other at exactly the same time.

We have to talk, man. We have to talk.

Todd stared at his cousin. He knew what secret he had to tell Soren. But what on earth did Soren have to tell him?

Chapter One

Sarah wasn't dead. She couldn't be.

Anna stood at the edge of her cousin's property and kicked at the ashes blackening the ground. The house was nothing but a charred frame, partially caved in. Not a breath of life, not a sign of movement but for a strip of faded police tape that fluttered in the breeze.

It had been three weeks since the fire, and everyone had given up on Sarah. But not Anna.

Her cousin wasn't dead. She knew it. She could feel it in her bones.

She'd given up trying to explain. She just knew, although she couldn't get anyone else to believe her. A feeling deep inside her soul was not exactly the kind of evidence the local police were looking for — if they were looking for evidence at all. They'd rushed through their investigation of a deadly arson series, more concerned with burying the bizarre events in the past than searching for the truth. Every time Anna suggested they follow up on a clue, they shook their heads.

Listen, honey. Your cousin was a nice girl. It's a terrible tragedy. But you have to accept the truth. She's gone. The others, too.

Anna kicked at a lump of ash then paced the edge of the property. Her aunt and uncle were gone. She'd shed plenty of tears over that awful fact. But her cousin wasn't dead.

Honey, we pulled three bodies from the house. Three.

She'd tried explaining that the third must have been Ginger, a relative from the other side of Sarah's family who'd been visiting at the time of the fire. But the authorities weren't interested in anything but a nice, quick wrap-up to the case.

The people of Black River need to heal. We need to move on.

That much, she got. The town was still reeling from the brutal attacks on three remote homesteads in the area. The Boone place had been burned to the ground along with the Voss lumber mill, located way out past the west end of town, as well as another cluster of houses at the edge of the woods to the south where the Macks family had lived for generations. The authorities still weren't sure how many people had died, and locals were so spooked, they only brought the subject up in whispers.

Anna didn't want to whisper. She wanted to scream. She'd driven out from Virginia the day she heard the news and had practically shouted at the state trooper who insisted her cousin was dead.

Sarah wasn't dead. She couldn't be.

She and Sarah had been as close as twins when they were kids, although as far as looks went, all they had in common was the green color of their eyes. Her cousin was a redhead, while her own hair was raven-black, but still, they liked to pretend they were twins. Even after Anna moved to the East Coast in third grade, they had remained close. Almost telepathically close, because she would phone Sarah exactly when Sarah was about to call her, already knowing whether her mood was up or down. They finished each other's sentences and liked the same things — like dogs and horses and autumn leaves. Every summer as a kid, Anna visited Montana and slept in the top bunk in Sarah's room, and they would stay up half the night chatting away. About everything, like hopes and dreams and somedays that seemed so bright, so full of possibility. They'd vowed to hike the tallest peaks together. To tame wild horses. To open a wildlife rescue center someday.

When Anna's parents had announced they were leaving Montana for Virginia all those years ago, her world had come to a crashing halt. When her father passed away soon after of cancer, and her mother up and found a new man, it felt the same way. But now, she really knew what a crashing halt felt like.

It was this sick-in-the-stomach feeling that overwhelmed her every time she stopped at the charred hulk that used to be her home away from home. She'd always vowed she'd move back to Montana someday — but Jesus, not like this. Not like this.

Honey, you need to move on, too. Go home to Virginia.

Home wasn't Virginia. Home was the sleepy town of Black River, Montana. And she sure as hell wasn't leaving until she uncovered the truth. She'd taken an indefinite leave of absence from her job on the East Coast to find her cousin. Somehow.

There were no survivors, honey. Not unless you count that bear.

Bear? What bear? She'd just about taken the detective by the shoulders and shaken him. Was he mocking her? Making a bad joke?

That grizzly we found half-dead on the lawn of the Boone place. Damnedest thing.

She rushed to the wildlife rescue center the second the police officer mentioned it, even though he shook his head hopelessly.

That grizzly's probably dead by now. No way can an animal survive wounds that bad.

But the bear had clung to life, as she discovered when she arrived at the rescue center. She knew the place since she and Sarah had volunteered there every summer. That was probably the only reason they'd let her in when she turned up after hours, asking about the bear.

"The poor thing," the rescue center director, Cynthia, told her. "He's been badly burned and severely wounded by wolves that mobbed him that very same night."

Wolves?

"Never heard anything like it," Cynthia said. "But old man Haggerty swears he saw a pack of wolves mauling the bear right beside the fire. They ran off when the fire trucks arrived."

"Can I see him?" she asked in a warbly, barely-holding-back-tears voice.

The tears were for her cousin and aunt and uncle, but somehow, that bear became a surrogate for them. From one breath

9

to the next, all her desperate hopes jumped over to him. He had to survive. He had to!

"We doubt he'll last another night," Cynthia said as she led Anna to his cage.

That had been her first night back in town, and she'd spent it beside the bear. The folks at the rescue center had taken pity on her, bending the rules so that she could stay.

She'd cried when she saw him, a mess of blood and burns. Every breath the bear took was a pained wheeze. Every tiny movement came with a pitiful moan. Only a few patches of fur remained unmarred, but those were glossy and thick. A grizzly in the prime of his life. What had he been doing at the Boone place? How was he connected to the fire?

The giant lay close to the bars of the cage. Anna slumped down beside it, listening to his labored breath.

"Don't die. Please don't die," she whispered, letting her tears fall freely once Cynthia left for the night.

The bear, of course, didn't say anything, but she could see his ears twitch.

"Stay with me," she said, slowly reaching a hand through the bars to stroke his fur.

It was coarse and so dense, her fingers caught in it. A light, sandy shade of brown — as light as she'd ever seen a grizzly. She'd seen a few up in the mountains on summer hikes with her cousin, albeit from far away.

"Don't die," she urged when his breathing stuttered and weakened. "Not now. Not like this."

Tears streamed down her face as she pictured her relatives, trapped inside the house as it burned. No one deserved to die like that. Not a person nor an animal.

"Don't die," she whispered.

Her fingers swept softly over the one patch of fur that wasn't matted with blood or burns, and her voice shook. "Please."

Her eyes slid shut, and when she opened them, she remembered it was just a bear there and not her cousin in a hospital bed. But it wasn't just a bear. It was an innocent life. Surely he deserved to live, too?

She was desperate for him to survive, but God, what could she do to help the beast that the vet hadn't already tried? Human chatter probably didn't do much for a wild bear, but she kept talking anyway, imagining what might appeal to a bear and infusing her voice with those things. It felt a little silly, but she had to do *something*.

She closed her eyes and made sure she didn't just say the words. She thought them, too.

"Think of mountain meadows in spring," she whispered, imagining waist-high grasses dancing and swaying. "Think of a clear, cool summer creek." This part of Montana was full of them, and she and Sarah had splashed in plenty, jumping from rock to rock then swimming in the deepest sections to cool off.

"Think of berries growing thick in the fall." That was one of the things she'd missed most after moving to Virginia, so it wasn't hard to summon the feeling that went with it. That semi-urgent, semi-sleepy, winding-down-to-winter feeling. The sweet pop of berry after berry in her mouth, the juice sticky on her hands. The succulent scent, wafting on a breeze.

"Just think of all the things you'll live to enjoy again," she pleaded. "Stay with me."

Such a beautiful animal couldn't — shouldn't — die in a cage. He should live. Thrive. Find a mate, make sandy-furred cubs, and live to a ripe old age somewhere way out in the deepest, densest forest where nobody would ever bother him again.

"Don't die..." Her voice grew drowsy. At some point, she withdrew her arm but continued mumbling until she'd dozed off in a heap next to the bear. The creak of a door startled her awake in the wee hours of morning when Cynthia and the vet came to make their rounds.

"Still alive?" Cynthia asked in surprise.

Anna studied the bear closely, terrified at how still he'd become. But then his chest expanded with a breath that was slightly less rattly than before, and hope seeped back into her soul. He was alive, thank goodness. But for how much longer?

The folks at the wildlife center let her keep visiting, and she spent days alternating between her vigil at the bear's side and wandering around town, trying to piece together the truth about the fire.

"My cousin didn't have any enemies. Why would someone want to burn her house down?"

The police shook their heads sadly. "A lot of crazy folks out there. You never know."

Looked like they'd never know, either. Not at the snail's pace of their investigation.

Anna followed any and every lead she could find, but none led to any hard facts. She might have hung her head and gone back to the East Coast after a week if it weren't for two things. First, a family who kept a seasonal cabin on the edge of town asked her to housesit.

"Always better to have someone keeping an eye on the place, especially after all those fires," they'd said.

Of course, that hadn't helped the Boones or the Vosses or the Macks family on the south side of town, but Anna kept her mouth shut. She welcomed the chance to stay in town to find out what she could. She could also afford a little time-out from the real estate business, having just sold two homes.

Second, the bear. The longer she stayed, the more she wished for his recovery. Desperately. One uncertain week became two, and midway through the tenth day, he opened his eyes and looked at her. Right at her.

It was only for a second, but her heart just about leaped out of her chest.

His eyes were the purest, brightest blue she'd ever seen, like a mountain lake shining under the noontime sun. Deep, intelligent eyes that held something special. Something... human almost. They were grateful. Weary. Curious yet pained at the same time, as if the bear wasn't only suffering from physical wounds. And they focused directly on her. Studying her. Wondering. Wishing, almost.

A moment later, his gaze grew unfocused, and he nodded off into an uneasy slumber. But Anna sat staring at him for a long time, full of shock and wonder. A single second of eye contact had never affected her that way, ever. Not the prettiest eyes of the sweetest deer foal, like the one she and Sarah had helped nurse back to health one summer. Not the bright, proud eyes of the old Clydesdale who used to nicker when she jogged by his Virginia farm. Not even her grandmother's eyes that had remained bright and fiery to the last.

Her heart beat faster, harder. Her fingers tightened around an invisible handhold.

She spent the rest of the day wondering why her body and soul wanted to dive back into the moment to relive that unexpected burst of wonder.

She talked to the bear every day, but at some point, she realized he didn't react to noise. When a door slammed, she'd jumped in surprise, but the bear didn't flinch. Clapping didn't draw his attention, nor did the barks or squawks of new arrivals to the rescue center.

Cynthia grew morose when Anna pointed it out. "Even if he survives, it's going to be hard to rehabilitate him to the wild. A deaf bear?"

Anna didn't want to ask what the alternative was. A proud animal like that belonged in the wild, not as a permanent captive of a wildlife center.

A day later, he looked at her again with those mesmerizing blue eyes, and she nearly cried at the message coded in them.

Help me. Please. Help me get out of this place.

It brought her right back to all the times as a little girl when she imagined living on a Doctor Doolittle farm where she could be friends with animals who were happy and free. She'd have a friendly lion, a playful tiger, a wolf who could tell her what every howl meant, and yes, a cuddly bear. A big one, like him.

But life didn't work like that, and much as she wanted to, she couldn't just set him free.

"You're hurt," she whispered through the bars of the cage.

Please, his eyes begged. *I have to get out of here.*

"You need a while longer to heal."

Although he was barely fit to sit up, he grew agitated, pacing and turning in his too-small cage, testing the bars with paws the size of dinner plates then crumpling in a heap.

It broke her heart, but what could she do? Even if she dared do the unthinkable, how would she actually manage it? You didn't just pop a cage gate open when no one else was around and wave an injured grizzly toward the door saying, *That way, buddy. Good luck and Godspeed.*

A padlock kept the bear's cage firmly closed, and it was only taken off when the bear was ushered from the front section to the separate back area so the cage could be cleaned. One of the assistants would duck in, change the straw bedding, fill the water, and back out again, then bolt and lock the cage.

Except for the day when the assistant slid the bolt but left off the lock. Anna opened her mouth, and the words were right on the tip of her tongue. *You forgot the lock. I'll get it for you.*

But her hand froze on the way to picking it up when she felt the bear's gaze on her. A gaze so intense, her skin prickled and warmed.

She met his eyes. His gaze pierced her, and not a hair on his body moved. Something pulsed between them. An understanding. A plan. A promise.

Yes, she was going out of her mind. But hell, it sure felt like that.

"Hey, Anna?" the assistant called.

Anna dropped her jacket over the lock lying beside the cage and whirled like a thief caught in the act. "Yes?"

"Time to close up. Want to help?"

"Sure," she said, much too quickly. "Sure."

They went around checking every window and every door, and Anna was thorough in every respect but replacing the lock on the bear's cage. Then she grabbed her jacket and watched him from the light switch at the far side of the room.

The bear sat studying her then dipped his chin in something startlingly close to a nod.

Her hand shook as she turned off the lights, and when she stepped outside and locked the front door, she shook her head at herself. She wasn't the accomplice to some secret crime. She was slowly losing her mind.

And she was kidding herself. She wasn't going to solve the mystery of her cousin's disappearance, and she wasn't going to save a wild bear. She was going to pack up the few things she'd brought and head back to Virginia the very next day. She'd get real, stop wishing, and accept the truth. Her cousin was dead. The bear would be taken care of by the authorities. And that was that.

She tried forcing the truth into her mind by repeating those words all the way back to the house she was staying in, all through dinner, and late into the night. She tapped the bed-sheets for an uneasy hour, telling herself it was time to admit defeat. Waking at the crack of dawn, she faced her bleary-eyed reflection in the mirror. The restless hours of sleep had exhausted rather than refreshed her, but she knew what she had to do.

Get real, Anna. It's time to get real. Go home. Mourn Sarah. Forget about that stupid bear.

And then her phone rang.

And rang and rang. Urgently, as if it knew what the message was.

"Anna?" Cynthia was breathless by the time she answered. "We need you right away."

Her heart raced into a sprint.

"What happened?"

"The bear is gone. Did you notice anything before you left yesterday?"

She answered quickly and lied so effortlessly, she shocked herself. "No."

"Nothing?"

"Not a thing."

Chapter Two

Anna did go back to the East Coast, though it took her a few days longer than she thought. When she got to Virginia, she did exactly what she'd promised herself: she got real, mourned the death of her cousin, and forgot about that poor, injured bear.

Well, okay. Two out of three wasn't bad.

She did get real. She went straight back to showing and selling homes. She did mourn her cousin, shedding tears just about every day and every night — and every time in between when some little memory would pop out of nowhere and make a mess of her emotions again.

But she didn't forget about the bear. She didn't want to forget about him. And how could she, given the mysterious circumstances of his disappearance?

She'd seen it with her own eyes the morning she'd rushed to the wildlife center after Cynthia's call. The cage stood wide open. The back door was open, too. No signs of damage, no claw marks.

"I don't understand it." Cynthia had fretted, pacing back and forth. "The lock is just lying there. The bars of the cage are untouched. But the bolt was just slid open like the bolt on the back door. The front door was locked from the outside. How could a bear possibly get out?"

Anna had looked around, gaping.

"The doors were locked when I left last night. I know they were," she'd stammered. Okay, the padlock to the bear cage hadn't been, but she left that part out. And anyway, Cynthia was right. No way could a bear slide the bolt to the cage.

"I can't understand it. What happened?"

Anna had no clue. She still had no clue, months later. She'd even called Cynthia a few times, asking whether the bear had been seen, but the answer was the same every time.

"Not a sign of him. It's the craziest thing," Cynthia said.

Anna mulled it over every morning and every night. Would she ever discover the truth?

The paperwork for her aunt and uncle's property in Montana came through, and though it made her sick, she signed off on the deed transfer, accepting the property as next of kin. Although she'd tried to accept her cousin's death, signing the property deed made all the doubts come back, along with the niggling feeling in her heart. What if Sarah wasn't dead? The evidence hadn't been conclusive, after all. And the feeling of Sarah being out there somewhere never quite went away. Some nights, Anna reached for the phone, sure it was about to ring with a call from Sarah. A few times, it had felt so real, so strong. First came the times when she was sure Sarah would call and cry for help — as though she'd survived the fire but was on the run from some evil force. Then came a time when Anna was sure Sarah would call and beg for her advice. Heart-to-heart advice, the way Sarah had once done when her boyfriend, Soren, had broken up with her. More recently, Anna reached for the phone with a smile when she sensed that her cousin had good news to share.

Which was crazy. She was just imagining things, right?

When the phone rang one night, she all but jumped to answer it, but it was Cynthia, not Sarah.

"Hi, Anna. How are you?"

Going crazy, I think.

"Fine. How are you?"

"Doing fine, sweetie. Listen, some folks have been asking about the land. Will you consider selling it?"

Anna sucked in a deep breath. It would kill her to sell that property, just as it would kill her to go back.

"No. Not selling. Not now."

Cynthia sighed. "Yeah, I can understand. Too much a part of your family."

18

Anna nodded into the phone. "I still can't believe they're gone."

Cynthia sighed deeply. "I know, honey. I feel the same way sometimes. Just last week, Sally James got back from Arizona. They're looking to retire down there. Can you believe that?"

"Well, I guess the winters aren't quite as harsh down there."

"Anyway," Cynthia went on, "Sally said she stopped in this cute little café where she swore she saw Jessica Macks. Craziest thing."

"Who's Jessica?" The name rang a bell, but that was it.

"Jessica Macks from the place south of town. The place that was burned down."

Anna froze. "She saw Jessica alive?"

Cynthia sighed. "You know how it is. You think you see somebody, but then you're not sure."

Her heart pounded in her chest. "Did Jessica know Sarah?"

"Around here, everyone knows everyone. But yes, I guess they did know each other. Sarah was always hanging around that Voss boy. What was his name?"

"Soren," Anna said immediately. The love of Sarah's life. Or so she'd thought before he left her.

"Right, Soren. His brother Simon and Jessica were a thing for a while, too."

"Where did Sally see her? When?"

"Honey, don't get your hopes up. Sally's eyes aren't that good. I shouldn't have mentioned it."

But her hopes were already up. Soaring, in fact. If Jessica was alive, maybe—

"Where? When?" she demanded.

"Last week, some place in central Arizona."

Within ten minutes, Anna had called Sally James, downloaded driving directions, and hit the road for her second cross-country trip of the past few months. She spread the map across her lap and glanced at it as she drove. All she had to do was follow I-40 west, right?

Two thousand miles west, but she didn't blink an eye. She had to be sure. If Jessica was alive, Sarah might be, too.

∞∞∞∞

"The Quarter Moon Café? Right down the street." The man in the hardware store pointed. "They've got the best muffins in town."

"Best wraps, too," the man ringing up his purchase added.

"Can't go wrong there," a third man agreed.

Anna sure hoped so. She'd tried settling her nerves, but it just didn't work. Especially not after a marathon drive with only short catnaps in the back seat of her car. Her back ached, her fingers twitched, but her hopes soared dangerously high.

It might not even be Jessica. And even if it was, she might not know anything about Sarah. Still, Anna felt one step closer to finding out some detail of her cousin's fate.

"Better hurry, though," the man added. "They close soon."

It was all she could do not to run, though she managed to keep to a race-walk. Every nerve in her body hummed with tension, and she clenched and reclenched her fists. She nearly walked into the wrong place, because there was a bar with a carved sign over the door that read, *Blue Moon Saloon.* She paused with one hand on the swinging doors the second she realized she'd stopped one door too soon.

The saloon doors burst open, and a man nearly bowled her over. She stumbled backward, and he pulled up, barely catching himself — and her — before sprawling to the ground. He clutched her by both arms and settled her hastily on her feet.

"Sorry," he said. Nearly shouted, in fact, the way a person wearing headphones shouted instead of using a normal speaking voice. His eyes flashed, and—

Anna froze as he hustled onward at a hectic trot.

Blue. His eyes were so blue.

She stood like a deer in headlights, stuck on that one thought that echoed over and over in her mind. Like a broken record, it circled around and repeated again and again. *Blue. So very blue.*

A thousand synapses fired, but none of them set off a rational thought.

20

Those bright, beautiful eyes that were so familiar. So honest. So true. Where had she seen him before?

She turned slowly, watching his broad back as he hurried across the street.

"Watch out!" she shouted.

A truck beeped and hit the brakes, but the man didn't even turn his head.

Wait, she wanted to yell after him. *Wait.*

She didn't even know what she wanted him to wait for. Only that it seemed imperative that he didn't leave now. She even took half a step in his direction before catching herself. What was she doing, following a stranger when she was supposed to be—

The saloon door swung outward, nearly clipping her in the ribs, and a woman burst out.

"Todd!" She knocked into Anna as if she didn't see her there, and just like Anna, she took one step toward the street before stopping and giving up her chase.

Anna glanced over. No wonder the woman hadn't seen her. Her eyes were full of tears.

The woman turned and noticed Anna for the first time. "Oh, sorr—" She broke off with a choked, squeaking sound. "Anna?"

Anna gaped. "Sarah?"

They stood there, staring at each other, before falling into an embrace.

"Oh my God, Sarah," Anna murmured, hugging her tight. "It's you. It really is you."

Sarah clutched her close, and tears wet Anna's shoulder. "Anna? Anna?"

Neither of them could eke out a coherent word. Anna let Sarah go just long enough to check that she wasn't dreaming. It was Sarah — Sarah with her emerald eyes and fiery red hair. Anna pulled her cousin close again and hugged her tight. God, Sarah was alive. Alive! She looked good, too — tan and bright and healthy. Maybe even better than she'd ever looked before.

"Sarah, I'm so glad to see you. God, am I glad to see you. Everyone said you were dead."

The saloon doors stirred, but Anna didn't move. Whoever it was could wait. Her cousin was alive!

A baby cooed, and Sarah pulled away quickly to reassure it. A big man stood taking up most of the space in the saloon doorway, making the baby in his arms look positively tiny. His stony face was terrifying to behold, though Sarah didn't seem intimidated. She murmured something as she took the baby and wiped the tears from her face.

"Anna, believe me, I'm so happy to see you. But I need a minute. Just a minute. We just got some pretty shocking news, and..."

Anna looked from her cousin to the man and the baby then back again. Wow, Sarah had a baby. And wow, Sarah had Soren, the man she'd loved for so many years. Which was great, but why did they both look so stricken?

"Sure," Anna managed. The air practically crackled with tension, and she backed away. "No problem. I'll just...um, wait in the park."

There was a park just across the street and down the block, a swath of green in the midst of a parched western landscape.

Sarah caught her by the arm and gave her a quick hug before letting her go. "I'm so sorry. I'll catch up in a minute."

"No problem." Well, obviously there was *some* problem, but the main thing was that Sarah was alive. And not only alive, but a mom.

Anna headed to the park, reeling inside. Had Sarah been in Arizona the whole time?

She looked around. It was a town right out of an old Western movie, full of boxy buildings with false fronts. Towering elms shaded the park, and Anna half expected the rattling sound coming down the street to be that of a covered wagon. It turned out to be just a dusty pickup piled high with bags of feed, but that fit, too. A bronze statue of a horse and rider stood at the head of the park, looking ready to bolt into the hills. They were so lifelike and full of energy she looked twice. An imposing stone building took up the center of the park, surrounded by a sea of green dappled with golden light.

The saloon she'd bumped into Sarah at wasn't the only old-fashioned place in town. There was a whole row of bars and stores, including a barbershop with a striped pole. Flags hung from lampposts — American flags alternating with the starburst flag of Arizona — all rippling gently in the breeze. At street level, the air barely stirred, but there was still a fresh, mountain feel to each breath she gulped, thanks to the surrounding hills thick with a forest of pines.

If it hadn't been so strikingly pretty, Anna might not have registered the town at all. Her mind was too busy with the thought of her cousin.

Sarah. Alive, one part of her brain repeated time after time.

All that blue. That bright, bright blue, another part whispered.

She didn't try to make sense of it all. She just walked and let snippets of emotion zip through her head.

Sarah. Baby. Soren.

And blue. That incredible blue.

It was lunchtime, and the park was dotted with people. Some in skirts or suits, others in cowboy hats. Walking on autopilot, she sat down at the end of a bench and stared into the distance.

If Sarah was alive, why hadn't she been in contact? Could it be that Sarah didn't want the world to know?

Anna looked around. Maybe she was just paranoid. Maybe there was a perfectly good explanation for all this — one Sarah would share just as soon as she sorted out whatever problem had cropped up.

She closed her eyes and tilted her head up toward the sky. Maybe that was the blue her mind was obsessing about. If she cracked her eyelids open just a bit, she could see patches of it through the trees.

A car backfired somewhere down the street, and she whipped her head around. The leaves rustled, and she took a deep breath, trying to settle her nerves. She'd just driven two-thirds of the way across the country. She'd just found her cousin. She could finally calm down, right?

But there was something making her jumpy. Something that wouldn't let her soak in the peace radiated by the trees.

She'd been vaguely aware of the man sitting at the far end of the bench when she sat down, but she only glanced over now. He was hunched over, his head hidden by his knees. Not so much in a drank-too-much-yesterday position — more like a quarterback after a play gone wrong. He barely moved except for his left boot drilling into the earth, grinding pebbles into dust. The plain gray T-shirt he wore stretched across his broad back, and his hands clutched at his hair.

Apparently, her cousin wasn't the only one having a rough day.

"Are you okay?" she ventured, relieved to pull her thoughts out of the seething cauldron of her mind.

The man didn't move, which ought to have been her signal to leave him alone. Even when she tore her gaze away from the thick lines of muscle bunched under the shirt, something pulled her back, and almost without realizing it, she scooted closer along the bench.

"Hey," she said softly, leaning out to catch his gaze.

His hair was short and sandy brown. Almost golden brown, in fact, like the leaves overhead. It was just long enough to give his fingers something to hang on to. Mussed, too, as if he'd worked through the night and hadn't gotten around to checking how it looked. And his hands — man, they were the size of bear paws. Big and clenched tight, like he didn't want to relax in case it meant losing his mind.

It made her ache just to see a man as anguished as that, and without thinking, she laid a hand on his shoulder. Which would have been asking for trouble if he'd been one of the down-and-out types who ghosted through public parks. But he was too young for that, too clean. He smelled of the woods, not alcohol, and the slump of his shoulders said he'd just received terrible news. A friend killed in a car accident, perhaps? A buddy killed far away in a senseless war?

"Are you okay?" she repeated.

His shoulder was round with muscle, and her hand just about slipped off. Then he looked up, and her breath caught.

24

It was the guy who'd nearly bowled her over at the saloon door. The one with incredible blue eyes. She'd barely gotten to process them before, but she was swimming in them now. They pulled her gaze in and wouldn't let go.

Warm, her mind decided. *Safe.*

Her thoughts were reduced to single-word sentences, and three more observations hurried on the heels of the first. *Sad. Betrayed. Hurt.*

And then came the one that made her heart skip. *Mine,* her mind announced. *Mine.*

Chapter Three

When Todd first sat down on that park bench, he'd sat down hard.

A son. He had a son?

The air whooshed out of his lungs, and his gut folded in on itself. Even sitting there on the park bench, he couldn't get his lungs to function properly. One breath would tangle with the next, just like the blood rushing through his veins.

He had a son, but he didn't have a son. The baby was Soren's now.

Jesus, the past two hours seemed so surreal. One minute, he'd been lumbering through the woods alone. The next, Soren had coaxed him out of bear form, into some clothes, and driven him into a dusty western town. Todd barely noticed the scenery, though, with his thoughts focused entirely on what he'd say to Soren when he had the chance. How the hell did you tell your cousin you accidentally slept with his mate?

As it turned out, Soren did most of the talking — aloud and into his mind at the same time — and Todd was the one who'd been swaying on his feet, unable to believe.

A year ago... East Coast... I missed Sarah so much that I couldn't help thinking about her... I never thought the old legends were true...

It sounded a lot like an apology, which had confused the hell out of him. Why was Soren apologizing?

His cousin had still been stumbling from one breathless explanation to the next when Sarah came into the room with a baby in her arms. At first, her face brightened with joy and gratitude, but then it clouded with concern.

Nice baby, he'd said, wondering why the tension in the room was crackling as wildly as an approaching thunderstorm. Wondering what Soren was getting around to. *Congratulations.*

Soren looked at Sarah, and Sarah looked at the ground.

We named him Ted, Soren said, running a hand over the baby's back in a gesture that was one hundred percent fiercely protective Papa Bear. Almost as if warning Todd off, which was crazy because Todd would never do anything to harm any child, let alone a member of his clan. *He's four months old.*

Nice.

Four months, Soren repeated slowly. *Born in July.*

Todd had never seen his cousin looked so pained. Was something wrong with the baby?

Soren swirled a finger in the air, telling Todd to do the math. Four months old and born in July meant the baby had been conceived back in...

His mind clicked over months and landed in October of the previous year.

October. Soren nodded, looking decades older than ever before.

At first, Todd wondered why the date mattered so much, and then it hit him.

Holy shit.

Todd locked his knees before they gave out from under him. Last October, Soren had been away, and he'd given Todd the task of keeping Sarah safe. And he had. He'd given up everything — his usual routine, his friends, his working hours — to keep his promise to Soren. And while he liked Sarah, he'd never regarded her as anything but his cousin's mate. She was totally off-limits — limits he would never dare cross and never had been interested in crossing.

Except that one night when something had gotten into Sarah, and by the time he got her away from the techno bar he'd pulled her out of, that *something* had taken over him, too. One minute, he was in man-on-a-mission, bodyguard mode, and the next...

He closed his eyes, wishing he could will reality away.

The next minute, he wasn't in charge of his body any more. He was vaguely aware of what was happening — and utterly, painfully aware of how wrong it was — but he was powerless to stop. Like a marionette, he followed the commands sent to his body by some outside force and marched straight over the invisible line he'd sworn to never, ever cross.

Afterward, he barely remembered the act, only snapping out of it and all but dying of shame.

And now, a situation that couldn't possibly be worse had just flipped right over to...to...this. He hadn't just screwed his cousin's mate. He'd fathered her baby. The baby cooing so innocently in her arms.

His baby.

He stared at the threadbare carpet in the back room of the saloon. He scratched at the jeans Soren had loaned him, wondering what to do or say. Finally, he forced himself to raise his eyes to Soren and face up to facts like the man he'd been raised to be. His jaw was locked, but even that didn't leave him with a way out because he could send his thoughts into his cousin's mind. He had to. He'd done wrong, and the only thing left to do was own up to it. Not to make excuses but somehow try to explain.

But how the hell would he explain, when he didn't understand it himself?

I never meant for it to happen, Soren. And it wasn't Sarah's fault, either. It was like something—

He'd expected Soren to cut him off with the outraged bark of an alpha, not with a single word whispered in his mind.

Moonlust.

Todd took a step back and stared.

Moonlust, Soren said again. *That night, I was thinking about Sarah, and somehow...*

Moonlust? Todd swayed a little on his feet. Moonlust was one of those legends old folks loved to talk about. The power that mates had to reach out to each other over great distances to touch and love and unite. When a wish became an action that played out not just in the mind, but in the body. When two lovers could feel each other, hear each other, and reconnect.

29

I never knew it could influence someone else, Soren said. *I shouldn't have let it happen.*

Todd stared. His cousin really was apologizing.

It was my fault, Soren went on.

Mine, too, Sarah added, her voice tight and trembling in his mind. She clutched the baby harder, and the shadow of fear colored her face.

Fear? Why would she ever be afraid of him?

One look at Soren, whose face had folded into fierce lines, told him why.

They're afraid we'll want the baby, his bear whispered inside.

I love this baby, Soren all but roared. He didn't say it aloud or voice the notion in Todd's mind, but his body sent out ferocious vibes all the same. *I'm never giving him up.*

Todd didn't want him to give up the baby. Why would he? That baby was theirs. A baby born of Soren and Sarah's love. He was just the...the...

Jesus, what did that make him?

Nobody, not in an equation of one plus one makes three.

Pain deeper than any he'd ever felt from any wound seeped into his bones. That baby wasn't his in the way that truly counted. He hadn't even known there was a baby until now. And yet, it felt as if something had been ripped from him. A piece of his soul, taken away.

I owe you everything, Soren said, shedding some of the tough alpha veneer he carried around like armor. *You saved my mate. You gave us a future we never thought we'd have.*

Soren didn't actually say, *You helped create the son I adore,* but Todd could see it in the lines of his brow. Along with the worry. *Please, please, don't try to take him from me. Don't make this a fight it doesn't have to be.*

What was he supposed to reply? That all the fight had gone out of him? That it would never have occurred to him to claim that child? He would never, ever break up a family. And hell no, he wouldn't pick a fight with Soren. Soren was family, and Sarah was Soren's mate. Todd had had no business getting between them in the first place.

Besides, what did he know about babies, other than the fact that they belonged with their parents?

Doesn't take much, he remembered his grandmother saying. *A little feeding, a lot of holding. A lot of love.*

Yeah, well. He was pretty sure it wasn't that simple. And deep inside, he knew that, even if Sarah slipped Teddy into his arms now, holding him would feel wrong. That was Soren and Sarah's child, not his.

"Todd," Soren called into his mind.

He shook his head and studied the diamond pattern in the faded rug. Clearly, he should have died when he'd had the chance. Why was fate toying with him? Why make him endure a months-long trek here, only to be treated as an outsider? Worse, as a threat to his own clan. Why?

Without thinking, he started for the door. Fate had taken everything away from him. His family. His home. His purpose. A big chunk of his pride. It had permanently scarred his body. And as if that wasn't enough, now fate was taking away what he didn't even know he had.

A son.

He stumbled, barely able to see, to think, to react.

Todd! Soren called after him, but he kept right on toward the door.

Todd! Sarah pleaded, echoing her mate.

He strode out the front room of the saloon and burst through the doors. Harsh Arizona sunlight hit him like a spotlight, and he was sure he heard destiny's cruel cackle in the breeze. He bumped into someone and just managed to stammer an apology before rushing across the street. All he could think was *away.* He needed to get away. From fate. From reality. From everything.

God, he'd never felt so tired or so at a loss. All his life, he'd heard the stories about destiny and fate and a greater design. And damn it, he'd believed them. He'd done everything a good bear should do. He served his clan. Put others before himself. He'd toiled. Sacrificed. Respected. But the past year — and especially today — had slowly torn apart that sacred temple in his mind. Maybe there was no such thing as all-powerful fate.

Or if there was, fate was a cruel master, not the benign force he'd been suckered into believing in. He'd followed the rules all his life, not for his own reward, but because doing good was right.

But Jesus, was he wrong about that? About everything?

His shoes scuffed over asphalt, then over flagstones, then the cushioned surface of the park's lush lawn. He'd stomped halfway across the park before pulling up short. Where the hell was he going? Why?

It was like a plug had been pulled. The last scraps of energy, the last breath of fire went out of him, and he sank onto a bench, holding his head in his hands. He concentrated on breathing instead of thinking and on the inch of space between his face and his knees.

A son. Jesus, he had a son.

No, we don't, his bear mourned. *Soren does.*

He covered his eyes, trying to erase that thought with something else. A plan. He had to make a plan.

Like what? his bear demanded.

Maybe he'd head back to the woods, shift back into bear form, and stay that way. Forever, preferably. Being a bear was easier because the world boiled down to hot/cold, hungry/full, awake/asleep. Not a lot more. Bears were more about today than yesterday or tomorrow, right?

Deep inside his body, his bear growled in dissent. *I feel. I think. I hurt. Doesn't matter if I'm on two feet or four. That won't make this ache go away.*

He ran his hands into his hair and hung on, just to have something to hang on to.

His head felt like it was going to explode. He clenched his teeth and clawed at his scalp, trying to make it go away. That didn't work, though. Neither did rocking a little or breathing slower or faster or more evenly. Nothing worked.

Until a featherlight touch warmed his shoulder, and his racing heart slowed down a little bit. The next breath he took didn't bounce over the previous one. It just slid down his throat, and although the air was dry as a bone in this godforsaken place, it felt good. So he concentrated on that.

The feather moved, making his breathing stretch and slow down, matching the motion on his shoulder. His jaw unlocked, and his fingers retreated from the roots of his hair. Maybe he didn't have to tear it out today. Maybe things would be okay.

Something shifted by his side, and the only strange thing about it was that it didn't trigger a thousand alarms in his mind. His brain didn't ask who or why or what was responsible. It just... relaxed a little bit. The hammering inside his skull eased, replaced by a sound. A faint whisper, like a little tap into his subconscious, and he strained to hear.

"Are you okay?"

He caught it on the second or third time. Something about the voice was familiar, and he looked up.

Emerald eyes. Freckles. A mane of thick, dark hair. Pencil-thin eyebrows, and above them, wispy bangs that didn't quite cover lines of concern.

A woman. A woman who was familiar, somehow.

Her lips moved again, and he itched for a slow-motion, zoomed-in replay because it was that nice to watch.

Was he okay? Not really. But having her close made things a little more bearable, somehow.

His inner beast started pacing. Sniffing. Maybe even hoping.

"Sure. Fine." He wasn't sure if he really heard his own voice or just imagined it in his head. He was too busy watching her lips perk at the corners in a tiny dawn of a smile. Like daybreak in winter when the sun barely peeked over the mountains. When a deep layer of snow covered everything, making the world seem peaceful and soft.

"You sure?" She tilted her head.

He nodded. A cardinal swooped by, and it occurred to him that he couldn't hear it. A rusty old dump truck bounced down the street, and though he could feel the rattle and screech in his bones, it didn't register as much more than a faint scratch in his ears. A mom wheeled a baby stroller past, and the child was gesturing and moving its mouth, but he couldn't hear that, either. Every sound in his universe was switched off, except the voice of the woman beside him.

He could hear her. It was faint, but he caught every word. He could *feel* the words, too, because she had a way of putting meaning into sound with unconscious cues that some sixth sense helped him pick up on.

A long, quiet moment passed as he marveled at that fact. His bear made satisfied, rumbling noises that vibrated in his chest.

Mine. Mate.

Having her there brought such a calm over him, even his bear's words didn't stress him out.

"Hi," she whispered, suddenly shy. When she pulled her hand from his shoulder, he wanted to grab it and put it back. She twirled a finger in her hair for a moment then stuck her hand out, offering a shake. "I'm Anna."

A faint memory started elbowing its way through the crowded mess that his mind had become, hooting and hollering from the back. *I know her! I know her!*

"Hi," he whispered, wrapping his hand around hers and squeezing just enough to satisfy his bear's urge to claim while gently enough not to crush.

Careful, his bear hollered. *Don't hurt her. Protect her.*

It felt as if he'd been pulled out of a blizzard and thrown into a cozy cabin with a fireplace. He was dazed and content. The rest of the world felt distant and vague, but that was okay, too. Why not bask in this one hint of goodness for a little while?

He was about to close his eyes and do just that when an itch set in on the back of his neck. An itch that started to burn, especially when Anna's eyes caught sight of something behind him and went wide. That perfect, expressive mouth frowned, and her nostrils flared. The acrid scent of fear washed off her.

He jumped to his feet and whirled, scanning the scene. What had frightened her? What danger was out there?

Using his left hand, he guided her back a step, and with his right, he did his best to pull without actually yanking her behind his back. Every hair on his body bristled as he tested the air and searched for who or what it might be. The tips of his bear fangs pushed at his gums.

My mate! You back the hell off! his bear roared in challenge to whoever it was out there, threatening her.

He bared his teeth — human teeth, if barely. Who was threatening this woman? Why?

A street-cleaning truck inched down the road, brushes whirring silently. Two men in suits strode out of the courthouse in the center of the park, jabbering into their cell phones. A group of people walked down the sidewalk beyond them, a blur of color and shape. Which one of them had alarmed her? Why?

The breeze was at his back, no help in teasing out a scent. He narrowed his eyes and studied one face after another, working his way across the park. Then his head whipped around just in time to see a man turn a corner and disappear from view. An average-size man in average-type clothes and brown hair. Shifter? Human? Damn it, he had nothing to go on there, and much as he wanted to chase the ass down and rattle a confession out of him, he wasn't about to leave Anna alone.

He let out the loudest mental roar he'd ever tried, keeping it guarded — he hoped — from human ears while warning every shifter in a five-mile radius not to fuck with the woman behind him.

My woman! My mate!

"What did you see?" he demanded, turning back and taking her by both arms.

Her wide eyes darted between his face and the corner he'd seen the man disappear around.

"I'm not sure. Someone..."

He tilted his head to catch her words, then shook his head. He very nearly shook her, too, though he'd never, ever manhandle her. She was obviously faking a brave face — a forced smile he didn't buy for one minute.

"I was probably just imagining it." She shrugged, but the gesture was stiff.

Imagining what? he wanted to yell. What danger did she recognize? What enemy?

The breeze carried the distinct scent of alarmed bear from behind him. He turned to see Soren and Sarah hurry up.

What the hell happened? Soren barked into his mind. He took up position beside Todd, sheltering Anna and Sarah.

The two of them glared at the street corner long and hard. Almost hard enough to make the streetlamp uproot itself and flee, if a lamp were capable of such a thing. And for a moment, it felt like old times, when the two of them had worked together to keep their clan safe.

Todd took a deep breath, letting go of the last traces of animosity that had been clinging to his shoulders. Soren was family. Soren was clan. Nothing would drive them apart. Not even fate. They'd work together to wipe out any hint of trouble on their turf.

No, this wasn't Montana. He was painfully aware of that. But this was Soren's new turf, and Todd would defend it like it was his own.

Defend the turf, the clan, and most of all, the baby. He'd fight to the death if he had to.

He caught himself there and laughed bitterly. Death. That would be nice. Maybe he'd even get the real thing this time. He could leave this world forever in a worthy way.

But then something brushed his sleeve. He caught sight of Anna, and suddenly, he wasn't in any rush to greet death any more. Maybe life was worth living, after all.

"Do you know each other?" Sarah asked, looking between the two of them. Her lips moved, and though he didn't hear the words, she helped out by shooting them into his mind.

Anna stared into his eyes, and he stared back.

"I think so," she said. That, he heard loud and clear.

Her lips trembled as she said it, and a new scent hit his nose. The scent of a woman interested in a man. Not quite aroused, but not quite at rest. Wondering. Wishing. Hoping, just a little bit.

His pulse skipped. Yeah, he had the same feeling.

I think I know her. I'm sure I do.

The problem was, his memory was pretty hazy on a lot of things since he'd nearly been beaten to death. Had he met her before or after that? Was he imagining it?

He shook himself into action. It was time to finish what they'd started a short time ago. He wrapped his hand around hers — gently enough not to crush, but tight enough to satisfy his bear's urge to claim.

"I'm Todd."

"Nice to meet you," she said, looking at him as if she, too, was trying to place him.

He tried making sense of it all, but he couldn't think straight. Not with his bear humming and sniffing her scent deeply.

Anna. Mine. Mate.

Whoa. He tried throwing on the brakes, but his bear was already skipping around in glee.

Mate. She's my destined mate.

Chapter Four

"I'm sorry I didn't come sooner," Sarah said, pulling Anna aside by the arm.

Anna wasn't sorry. She just wanted to stay close to Todd. But Soren was leading him off in one direction, while Sarah steered her in another.

Did Todd feel it, too? The zing of energy that bounced between them when they'd touched? The painful stretch and popping sensation when he'd stepped away? The feeling that they had met before, and not just in passing?

He strode away, shoulder to massive shoulder with Soren, who could have been his brother, they were so alike. They had the build of lumberjacks and the confident step of predators who stood all the way up in the food chain. But while Soren definitely exuded *king-of-this-domain* vibes, Todd had a subtler, but equally powerful presence. She could see it in the way he moved, in the way he turned his head to scan the area, and in the way people scurried aside when he came near.

"Was something wrong?" Sarah asked.

"Wrong?" She'd never experienced anything that felt more right.

"Todd looked like he was about to kill someone, and you looked a little scared."

"Oh, um..." She tried waving it off, but the feeling was still there, along with the alarms in the back of her mind. Having Todd play bodyguard had pushed away the panic, but the little niggle was still there.

A man had been watching them from across the street. A man she knew from Montana.

A man she would have been happy never to see again.

He'd arrived in Black River a week after the fire and immediately started asking questions. Weird, personal questions not even the cops had posed, like which of the locals had been friendly with whom and whether any of the victims left behind boyfriends or girlfriends he ought to know about. Why the hell would a perfect stranger inquire about things like that?

She shivered, remembering the first time the man had approached her. Without so much as a *Sorry about the loved ones you lost*, he'd launched into an interrogation.

"I hear your cousin Sarah was friendly with one of the Voss brothers. Is that true?"

He was a fifty-something farmer type, unremarkable except for the pale, thin scar that stretched an inch straight up from his upper lip on the right side. It gave him a built-in smile, though his eyes never matched that look. They were a strange, pale gray and very angry. Ominous, almost, like a storm coming over the horizon.

The way he posed the question suggested an agenda she didn't even want to guess at, so she had shot back a curt answer before walking away. "Why does it matter? My cousin is dead."

A lie, because she'd been sure Sarah was alive, but suddenly, it seemed better not to share that with this man.

"It matters," he'd growled as she walked away. "Believe me, it matters."

Creep didn't begin to describe the guy.

She'd hoped he was just passing through Black River, but he rented a cabin and settled in. Asking questions and doing the weirdest things, like stopping by her cousin's burned-out house and kicking through the ashes. He'd spent a lot of time out by the charred remains of the Voss lumber mill, too, doing who knows what. She'd done her best to avoid him. But then he'd stopped by the wildlife shelter, asking about the injured bear.

"Can I see him?" She remembered hearing his scratchy voice in the lobby one day when she was in the back, checking on the bear.

40

Thank God for Cynthia putting her foot down. "This isn't a hospital and certainly not a circus. No visits."

"That bear's dangerous, you know," the man went on as if he hadn't heard. "Ought to be put down."

When Anna heard that, she stood abruptly to block the view to the cage. And not a moment too soon, because the man's piercing eyes had appeared at the glass window in the door separating the public part of the wildlife center from the back.

"Best thing for everyone would be to put a silver bullet in his head right now."

A silver bullet?

His tone said he wasn't kidding, and she'd just about marched out of the back room to give him a piece of her mind.

Lucky thing Cynthia had kept her cool. "Sadly, we don't think that will be necessary. He's likely to die any day now. Sorry, but we're closing now. Let me show you to the door."

That had been the only time he'd entered the wildlife center, but Anna had seen him parked outside a number of times. He'd left her a note, too.

If you hear anything more about your cousin or those Voss brothers, let me know. He'd left an out-of-state cell phone number and signed it Emmett LeBlanc.

She'd taken a match to the note and vowed to be careful what she said about Sarah from then on. Maybe it wasn't smart to insist Sarah was alive. Not if creeps like Emmett LeBlanc were interested.

The thing was, he seemed interested in everybody. Not just Sarah and the bear, but everybody in the town. He'd been asking about Jessica Macks, too — another woman who hadn't been seen since the arson attacks. The waitress at the town diner said he'd claimed to be a crime novelist looking for inspiration, but Anna didn't believe that one bit.

And anyway, that was months back and hundreds of miles away in Montana. This was Arizona. Sarah shot a glance across the street. She'd probably just been imagining things. That hadn't been Emmett. It couldn't be.

"Is everything okay?" Sarah asked, looking worried.

"Fine. Great." She turned back to her cousin and hugged her again. "I'm so glad I found you."

Todd and Soren had disappeared inside the saloon, and when Sarah led her in their direction, Anna's nerves jumped up and down in glee. But at the last second, Sarah waved her through another door to the café on the right.

"Quarter Moon Café," Anna murmured, reading the old-fashioned carved sign swinging over the door.

"Soren made it," Sarah gushed in the same tone she'd always enthused about the man she loved.

"It's nice you guys got back together," Anna said. Her cousin had been gutted by the breakup, but apparently things had worked out after all. "I'm so happy for you."

The sweet scent of berries and vanilla and fresh fruit hit her the second she stepped inside. The dark-haired woman behind the counter held Sarah's baby high and made his arm wave.

"See? I told you Mommy was coming back," she cooed.

Sarah beamed a mile wide and held her arms out. "Thanks, Jessica."

"Anything for my little Teddy Bear," the woman said, kissing him.

"Jessica, this is Anna. Anna, meet Jessica," her cousin said.

Jessica Macks? The one she'd been tipped off about?

"Hi," Anna offered, suddenly feeling very much an outsider. She and her cousin had always been close, but Sarah seemed to have started a whole new life that Anna played no part in. A man, a baby, a new job, new friends. . .

"And this is Teddy," Sarah said, showing off her baby.

A pang went through Anna, as it always did when she hadn't prepared herself for cozy mother-baby scenes. Most of the time, she was able to steel herself in advance, but sometimes, she wasn't ready, and the sense of loss would hit her out of the blue.

I was supposed to be a mom, too, a voice in the back of her mind murmured sadly.

She saw Sarah freeze and shoot her an apologetic look. Anna still had the little pink blanket her cousin had made for her, eight years ago. A blanket she never got to use because she'd miscarried that baby. She'd miscarried a second time, too.

She forced a smile. This was an occasion to celebrate, not a time to mourn something that wasn't meant to be. And clearly, Sarah and Soren were meant to be.

Anna tickled the baby's ruddy cheek and cooed. "Gonna be a big boy someday."

Sarah laughed, relieved. "That's for sure."

"Just like his daddy," Anna continued.

Sarah's face fell, and she wondered why.

"We're just closing up, but you're welcome to hang out for a while," Jessica said quickly.

They took a corner table, sipped tea, nibbled the best raspberry-chocolate muffins Anna had ever tried, and talked. About easy things to begin with, then the harder parts.

Sarah, it seemed, had moved to Arizona, hooked back up with Soren, and started all over again. Soren and his brother, Simon, ran the saloon next door, and Jessica ran the café. Sarah did the accounting for both places, just like she used to do for her parents' shop, and Jessica's sister, Janna, waitressed, too.

They were one big, cozy family. Anna bit back a wistful sigh.

That was the easy part of the conversation.

"What happened, Sarah?" Anna whispered when she was down to her last sip of tea. She hadn't overlooked the burn scars on her cousin's hands, nor the long, pink line where a flame had scored her forearm. "How did you get out?"

Sarah shook her head and hugged the baby closer.

"Sorry if you don't want to talk about it..." Anna rushed to add. "It's just that everyone told me you were dead, and I was so sure you weren't, but I didn't hear from you for so long..."

Sarah took a deep breath. "I'm so sorry. I knew I could trust you, but I didn't want to drag you into my mess."

"I'd help you with anything, Sarah. You know that."

Sarah's eyes grew distant. Frightened. "You couldn't have helped me. You would only have put yourself in danger, too."

Danger? Anna looked around. This place seemed so peaceful, so secure.

The sentiment must have shown on her face, because Sarah leaned in. "We're okay now. It's all good. But there was a scary time..." She trailed off, then recomposed her face and struck a cheerier tone. "We're good now. Everything is okay."

She looked like she truly meant it, so Anna didn't push the topic.

"I'm sorry for just turning up out of the blue. Seems like you've had a busy morning."

Sarah patted the baby's bottom and tucked a stray lock of hair behind her ear. "Yeah, you can say that. But God, it's great to see you."

Anna laughed. "It's great to see you."

"How did you find me, anyway?"

Anna told her about Cynthia's call and Sally James having spotted Jessica Macks — at which point the broom that had been whisking quietly behind them stopped abruptly. Sarah and Jessica exchanged worried looks but they didn't say anything, so Anna finished up with her drive from Virginia.

"You must be exhausted," Sarah said. "God, I'm such a bad cousin. Come on. Would you like a shower? A nap? How long can you stay?"

Anna laughed. She hadn't thought ahead to anything other than finding Sarah. Now that she was here, she had no clue. "Well, I could stay a few days if that's okay."

"You *have* to stay," Sarah insisted. "We have a lot of catching up to do. But first things first."

Sarah led her to the apartment on the second floor and shooed her straight into the shower. When she was done, Sarah led her back downstairs, out the back, and toward a separate building standing across the service lot behind the café and saloon.

"We'll set you up in the place above the garage. It's not much, but you'll have some privacy here."

The stairs creaked and dust rose as she walked, but when they came to the slope-roofed area above the garage, it was airy and cool.

"We've been meaning to fix it up, but I think it will be okay."

"It's great." Anna already loved the Navajo rug and the sunlight streaming through the dormers on the shady north side.

"There's a small living room in the front..." Sarah motioned as heavy footsteps sounded on the stairs behind them. "... a half-bath over here, and two little bedrooms in the back. You can have the one on the right."

Soren came lumbering into view, and it seemed he hadn't heard, because he was looking behind him, talking to someone else. "You can have the room on the left—"

Soren stopped short when he saw Anna. A second later, Todd appeared behind him. There was a lot of Soren taking up the landing, but there was plenty of Todd to take in, too. The sandy-brown hair was still mussed as if he'd raked his hands through it several more times. His face was lined and weary, but he brightened when she met his gaze. At least, she thought he did. Or maybe it was the light?

For a second, the squeak of the overhead fan was the only sound in that small space. That and the sound of her skipping pulse in her ears.

"Wait. I was just saying Anna could stay here," Sarah said.

"I just talked Todd into staying for a few days," Soren replied.

When Todd had just come up the stairs, he had looked reluctant. But now, he seemed to be just as eager as she was.

Sarah looked at her with a *wouldn't-that-be-awkward* look.

Awkward? Anna pursed her lips. Nope, it wouldn't be awkward at all.

"We can share," she said, trying far too hard to sound nonchalant. Wondering why she liked the idea so much. "That's fine."

She smiled at him, and the two of them fell into a half-dazed, gazing-into-each-other's-eyes state. She'd never seen eyes quite as blue and honest as his. Well, it felt like she had, but she couldn't put her finger on where or when.

"Okay with me," he whispered.

She nodded, holding her breath. "Okay with me, too."

Chapter Five

"You just got here. You can't leave."

Todd shook his head. Soren kept saying that, but Todd wasn't sure he should — or even could — stay.

"Where else will you go? What will you do?"

He had no clue, but hanging around witnessing his cousin's newfound family bliss was definitely not the right place to be. How could he see little Teddy every day and not have his heart crushed?

"You have to stay, man," Soren went on.

Soren didn't seem to understand how much he was asking, and Todd wasn't sure he could endure staying. Until Soren walked him up to that little den of an apartment over the garage and he saw Anna again. She stared at him in surprise, and instead of thinking about what he might lose, he thought about what he stood to gain.

Mate. Mine. His bear jumped up and down inside.

His heart started pounding, the blood rushing through his veins.

Was it really possible? Did he really have a mate?

Her eyes sparked and her lips parted. Maybe even trembled until she caught her bottom lip with her teeth, a slim line of white peeking around the pink. When she caught a lock of hair and twirled it with her finger absently, he longed to reach out and twirl it, too.

Definitely my mate, his bear hummed inside.

God, she was pretty. And her emerald eyes were so clear, so genuine. Her smile was the only one in the room that wasn't forced, and her words were the only ones that reached his ears, perfectly clear and crisp.

"We can share," she'd said. "That's fine."

And just like that, sticking around Soren's place didn't seem like a punishment anymore.

More like a chance, his bear agreed. *One last chance.*

Last chance at what?

Of starting over again.

An idea that had seemed utterly impossible until now.

Quickly, before Soren or Sarah could protest, he chimed in. "Okay with me."

Anna nodded quickly. "Okay with me, too."

Which seemed so easy at the time, but it was bound to turn into torture of a completely different kind. Anna was human. She didn't know about destined mates or bears — or any other kind of shifter, for that matter. Plus, he still couldn't place her, and it seemed really important to figure that out.

Just when he was about to give in and start on the first of a thousand questions he wanted to ask — like, *Anna, is your hair as soft as it looks?* Or, *Anna, can I trust you with the truth about who I really am?* — Sarah called her away.

Then Soren led him down the stairs and into the back room of the saloon, and Anna seemed a million miles away again. His bear sniffed in the direction she'd gone and whimpered unabashedly.

"Look. We could really use your help. Right here. You think you can put some life back into this wreck?" Soren motioned toward the dilapidated wooden bar.

It wasn't the masterpiece of woodwork that the hundred-year-old mahogany bar in the front room was, but it was solid oak and a nice piece of joinery.

"Some fool painted the whole thing black," Soren muttered, running a finger along one chipped edge. "But I reckon it would look okay if we got it down to raw wood. Varnish it up, make it shine."

Todd slowly looked up and down the length of the bar. It was a good twenty feet long and six inches taller than his six-foot frame. A two- to three-week job, at best. Was Soren really serious about him sticking around that long?

Soren nodded, and Todd cursed himself for not guarding his thoughts more carefully.

"Look, I don't want to make this any harder on you or us than it already is," Soren said.

You or us. Todd turned the words over in his mind. It made them sound like two opposing sides. But he wasn't his cousin's enemy. He'd always been Soren's most loyal ally. Had nothing changed — or had everything changed?

Soren shook his head vehemently. "The important part will never change. We're family, man. We stick together."

It sounded good, but Todd could sense the uncertainty in his cousin's words. Enough to make him realize that Soren had everything at stake: his mate, his son, the stability of his clan.

Soren let out a long breath. "We'll sort this out. Somehow. Sarah says we just need to give it time."

A century wouldn't be enough time. Not for him to make peace with himself. That part was easier for Soren. The baby was his in spirit and soul, and Todd would never contest that. But he'd always have to live with an empty space, knowing he had a son who could never be his own.

Soren cleared his throat and motioned toward the bar. "Look, we've been getting a lot of requests for private functions. If we get this back room fixed up, it would give us another income stream. Help us diversify a bit."

Todd had never considered his cousin much of a businessman, but it seemed Soren had stepped up his game. As the oldest grandson of the ruling alpha, Soren had been groomed to lead their clan, while his younger brother Simon was to take over the day-to-day workings of the family lumber mill. Todd's job was to support them as their most reliable go-to man. They'd always taken their responsibilities seriously, but it had always been a *someday* kind of thing.

Now, they'd all been thrust into a harsh new reality. Soren had obviously risen to the challenge. Simon, too. And Todd — well...

Stop feeling sorry for yourself and do the same, his bear barked.

Soren's head snapped up and left, away from him. "Teddy's waking up. I'll be right back."

Todd stared at the bar for a good long time after Soren disappeared upstairs. Then he grabbed a sheet of sandpaper and got to work on the surface in harsh, hacking swipes.

That was Soren's baby. Not his, and it never would be. But he'd prove himself a worthy uncle, damn it. He'd do his part to provide for this clan.

"Whoa. We've got an electric sander, you know," Simon said, coming up a few minutes later.

Todd stopped and looked at the patch he'd started to clear. Okay, so his test patch had turned into a test acre. He'd call that a warm-up and try to get his head screwed on right.

"Think you can make this thing shine?" Simon asked, more in challenge than in question.

They both looked over the bar. The surface was hopelessly pitted and stained, and the center section was cracked.

"Not sure," he murmured. "But I'll try."

He pictured the extra income going into things like a tricycle or a swing. Yeah, he'd try, all right.

Simon smacked him on the shoulder in an *attaboy* gesture and motioned with the muffin in his hand. "Let me just talk to Jess and finish the world's best muffin here. Then I'll help."

Todd drew a tight line with his lips. Soren had a mate. Simon had a mate...

I have a mate, too, his bear rumbled inside.

He gave the bear the silent treatment while he sealed the area off with sheets of plastic and tried not to think about Anna. A losing proposition, because he couldn't help but picture what she might be doing. Had Jessica put her to work, too? Did she enjoy it? How long was she planning to stay?

"Ready?" Simon asked, coming back into the room. The scent of his mate clung to his shoulders, evidence of the parting nuzzle they must have shared.

Todd stepped back and checked every inch of his work, then set about checking the filters on the sander. No way was he letting any dust reach Teddy's lungs. Then he nodded slowly and took a deep breath. Yeah, he was ready.

Somehow, he'd survive his stay in Arizona. He'd endure the proximity to the baby and formulate a plan for what to do next. Staying long term wasn't an option. So what would he do?

Maybe he'd head back to Montana. Maybe someplace new. . .

Our mate is here, his bear said.

He shook his head, turned on the sander, and let it screech against the wood.

∞∞∞

Working on the bar helped him get through the day. A day with so many ups and downs, it was like a roller coaster — and he hated roller coasters, like most bears. The saloon was closed on Mondays, so he'd been able to work through the evening, when Soren and Simon joined him for a quiet meal of barbecued ribs. Just the three of them, pretending it was like old times, even though it was anything but and never would be again.

He took a shower — a weird sensation, after having been in bear form for so long — then headed to the apartment over the garage, wondering if he even remembered what it felt like to sleep in a bed.

Anna was coming down the narrow stairs just as he was going up, and they both froze for a while.

God, her eyes were pretty. Her hair was so shiny, and that feeling that he'd met her somewhere, sometime hit him again.

"Hi," she whispered.

So far, he'd only been able to hear the others when they pushed their thoughts into his mind. But Sarah, he could hear perfectly.

Of course, his bear said. *She's my mate.*

"Hi," he said. He couldn't hear his own voice, and he hoped to hell it wasn't too loud.

"Did you have a good day?"

He didn't answer immediately, which probably gave him away, but Anna just waited patiently. No judging. Not the *oh-you-poor-bugger* look he got from Jessica, Simon, and the others.

"It was okay." Well, a lot of it had been hell, but there were bright spots, too — all of which involved her. "How about you?"

She nodded, glanced down, and when she looked back, her gaze slid to his lips. And all of a sudden, all he could think of was a kiss.

Her nostrils flared, and whoa, he wondered if she was thinking the same thing.

Without thinking — because how could he think when a powerful magnet was drawing on every cell in his body? — he leaned closer, and she leaned in, too. Her mouth cracked open as if she was imagining a kiss, too, and every nerve in his body bounced up and down.

Then the towel in her hand fell, making Anna blink, gulp, and motion down the stairs. "I was just on my way to the shower. It was such a hot day..."

Hot for sure, his bear hummed.

He didn't respond at first, because he was still imagining a kiss. But then he nodded and pressed his body against one wall. "Sure. Sorry."

The funny thing was, she looked sorry, too.

Me, three, his bear sighed.

She smiled, though, and when she squeezed past, her sweet scent just about knocked him over. He closed his eyes and drew a deep breath, filling his lungs with it. God, she was so close. So perfect. So...so...

Mine, his bear growled.

He was still there seconds later, motionless as a statue, when she stopped at the bottom of the stairs and turned back. "Goodnight, Todd."

He just managed to shake himself out of his daze and reply, "Goodnight, Anna."

Even her name felt perfect on his tongue.

And then she was gone. For a while, at least. Eventually, he heard her come back up the stairs and quietly tuck herself into the bed on her side of the thin partition wall. He lay in his own bed, barely moving. Barely breathing, except for testing the air for her scent.

He caught a whiff of it, and Jesus, it was torture, having her so close, yet so far.

Bust through the wall, his bear demanded. *I need her.*

Like that would convince her he was a guy worth having.

Go talk to her, then.

Talking. Right. Like he was any good at that kind of thing.

Show her we're worthy.

That only made him despair, because he wasn't worthy. His right hand didn't have one-tenth the range of motion it used to have, and he had burn scars down the side of his chest. Other scars, too, like the long, jagged one that went from his ribs to his hip where a rogue wolf had almost gutted him back in the ambush in Montana. He wasn't the bear he used to be. He'd never come close again.

So he didn't bust through the wall or talk to her or anything else. He just lay quietly, staring at the ceiling. What was he doing in Arizona, anyway?

He snorted and filled in the answer. Being screwed by fate, that's what he was doing.

Fate had been messing with him for months now — tricking him into fathering a child he'd never get to call his own, then allowing him to survive instead of dying an honorable death. Fate had taken away nearly every member of his family.

Clearly, fate was out to make him suffer in any way possible.

Which made his blood run cold. If Anna was his mate, fate could hurt her, too. That's the way fate seemed to work — with sneaky, below-the-belt punches aimed at the ones he loved. Jesus, if he allowed himself to get closer to Anna, what might fate do then? Strike her down with a bolt of lightning? Let her wither away with cancer?

He clutched and clawed at the bedsheets, covered in sweat. If fate was a tangible enemy — a bear, maybe, or a hellhound or even a dragon — at least then he could fight it head on. But he was powerless. Absolutely powerless against fate and its cruel games.

If Anna really meant anything to him—

She means everything, his bear growled.

—he'd have to stay away from her. He couldn't give fate another innocent victim to toy with.

He lay limp and sweating, gritting his teeth. Shit. Fate had already done that. Given him an incredible gift — Anna — only to whisk all hope away again.

He could practically hear fate's laughter waft by on the wind.

∞∞∞∞

That was just the first day, and the ones that followed were about the same.

Nights dragged by, one empty minute after another. An eternity later, dawn would tinge the horizon, coloring the white walls of his room with one shade of pink after another. The colors were bolder than those of a Montana sunrise, and they seemed to dare him.

Come on, bear. Show us what you got.

He'd flex and unflex the fingers of his right hand, wishing he could leave a claw mark across the wall.

Anna had offered to help in the café for the duration of her visit, so she always woke early, and though bears were usually sound sleepers, he never failed to wake up to listen to her tiptoe around. He'd lie perfectly still, fighting the urge to jump up and run over. To say good morning, to see her smile. Maybe even wrap her in his arms. It took every scrap of determination in his body to resist the call of her body, and his heart ached every time she padded down the stairs.

Mate, his bear hummed sadly. *Need my mate.*

Hanging around this place was going to kill him, but he had no clue where to go or what to do. He was only just getting used to walking around in human form, for Christ's sake.

Plus, Anna was in no hurry to leave, either. Which would only make things harder in the long run, but a part of him still rejoiced. He savored every brief encounter, every fleeting glance.

54

Like every time they passed on the narrow stairway and stared into each other's eyes.

Like when she brought him a drink or snack and gushed about whatever project he'd been working on.

"The bar is looking good," she'd say.

Bar? What bar? He needed a minute to drag himself back to his surroundings, every time.

Work on the bar could only proceed in the mornings when the saloon was closed. Anna had volunteered to help waitress there, too, which meant everyone was busy in the evenings except him. He needed more than just a morning job. He needed the feeling of contributing to the clan.

So he'd walked through the apartment over the saloon where the others all lived when they weren't working their tails off. The place had character, but it was run-down and badly in need of... well, everything. Especially a second bathroom, where progress had stalled because none of the others really had the time to devote to it.

Which meant he'd just found himself a job for those too-quiet afternoons. He sweated a new shower into place, laid tiles, and hooked up a shiny new sink. Two times out of three, his wrecked hand would slip or cramp, sending a bolt or clamp rolling across the floor. Glaring at his fingers didn't help, but he did it anyway, giving the patchwork of scars there the evil eye. Then he'd grit his teeth, collect the parts, and start all over again, just to prove to fate he could spite it in one tiny way.

Soren or Simon would stop by to help when they could, and it was a little like old times, working on a project side by side. For a while, he'd turn off the part of his mind that grappled with the present and let himself slip away into the past.

Then the baby would wake from a nap and cry out to be held, and part of him would cry, too.

Those were the times he actually heard Teddy. Other times, Soren would go rushing down the hallway like the house was on fire when Todd hadn't heard or sensed a thing.

"I didn't hear him, either." Simon once shrugged.

But Soren *always* heard the baby, no matter how close or how far he was. He knew when the baby was sleepy, when he wanted to play, when he needed to nurse. The man was so tuned in to that child, he beat Sarah to the crib at times. And if that didn't prove Soren was the father, what did?

Todd worked his jaw from left to right and contemplated the empty sink.

Sarah had been avoiding him, and in a way, he was okay with that because the situation was awkward for him, too. The fact that the one night they'd slept together was only a vague blur in his mind didn't help, nor did the knowledge that she'd been with Soren in spirit and not him. The worst part was that *you were just a puppet in destiny's machinery* feeling he couldn't quite stomach.

Think of something else. Think of something nice, he coached himself.

And *zoom*, his mind went right to an image of Anna, twirling a finger in her hair.

He forced the image away and replaced it with one of home. He closed his eyes, remembering Montana. The clean mountain air, the rushing creeks, the shady woods.

"You miss it?" he murmured.

"Miss what?" Simon asked absently, wearing his usual, blissed-out, *I love my mate and my life* look.

Right. Why would Simon miss Montana? He had a new life here, and it was a good one. Like Soren, Simon had settled down with a mate he adored. Business was booming in the saloon and the café. The only thing Simon didn't have was a cub of his own, but Todd suspected that wasn't far off — not seeing the way Jessica cuddled Teddy or the way Simon grinned while bouncing the little guy on his knee.

"My turn!" he'd protest when Janna tried to take Teddy away.

"My turn!" Jessica would chime in.

"My turn," Soren would cut in, cuddling the baby close.

Watching them made his soul bleed, but it warmed his heart, too. The baby was loved. Cared for. Protected by his clan. Just the way it should be. What else could he wish the baby had?

His bear rumbled inside, not satisfied. *Might not be ours to keep, but ours to help care for.*

But how? How was he ever going to do that?

A week passed with him alternating between sanding the bar and working upstairs, and everyone had oohed and aahed when the bathroom was done.

"Oh, my God. I love you," Janna said, squeezing into the room with everyone else. "I mean, I love Cole," she added, giving her mate a reassuring pat on the arm. "But in terms of bathrooms, you're my hero, man."

His bear heaved a sigh inside. Some hero he made.

But Janna was serious, and so were the others. Jessica even brought up a bottle of champagne and passed glasses around to everyone for a toast.

"You gotta celebrate the small stuff," she said with a wink.

Yeah, small stuff. Maybe he ought to get used to that.

"Great job," Anna agreed, holding her glass up to his. Their eyes met, and his heart just about jumped out of his chest with need.

Not need, he told his bear. *Greed. We can't have her. We have to keep her safe.*

"Now you can get to work on the deck," Janna quipped.

"Janna!" everyone scolded.

She put up her hands. "Well, he said he wanted work. . . "

Todd nodded quickly. He did. Back in Montana, he'd been busy all day, every day. Here, he was superfluous, and that was the hardest part. Teddy already had a devoted father and family. In fact, he wailed anytime Todd came close, which made the message loud and clear. *Get out of here, stranger. You make me feel unsafe.*

Christ, he would lay down his life for Teddy. He already had, in a way. And he'd do it again and again and again, not because he wanted to claim his son but because Teddy was clan.

And that was the only thing that kept him from wandering back into the woods and returning to life as a bear. That just-in-case feeling in the back of his mind. That feeling that evil could come crashing back into their world at any time.

That, and Anna. He just couldn't bring himself to abandon his mate. So he worshiped her from a distance. Followed her every move from afar. Sipped her scent and clung to it like a sailor clinging to a sinking ship. That was all he allowed himself.

That was all he dared take.

Chapter Six

Anna counted the days since she'd arrived in Arizona. Five?
Six? It was all a whirlwind, and her mind still spun with
everything that had happened.

She'd found her cousin alive and well. She'd met a man who
didn't cease to intrigue her — no matter how quiet he was or
how sweaty at the end of a hard workday. She'd been pitching
in to help with what seemed like the hardest working group
of people west of the Mississippi, and she loved every minute
of it. So much, she sometimes wondered if she ever wanted
to leave. There was such team spirit among her cousin's new
extended family, such drive. Being part of it gave her a greater
sense of satisfaction than she'd had for a long time. Luckily,
it was the slow season in the real estate market, so she could
take some time off. But she couldn't stay forever, even though
she sometimes wished she could.

Sarah and her friends made good company. The work was
honest. The baby was adorable. Plus, there was the perk of
sharing digs with Herr Hunksome, Todd. There was a certain
thrill to having him as a housemate. Despite the fact that
he kept things strictly platonic, the man carried a permanent
undercurrent of sexuality around. The second they got close,
a little hum would start up — the kind an electric fence made,
or a generator chugging somewhere in the distance. Whenever
she looked Todd's way, he'd avert those amazing blue eyes,
always a moment too late to hide that he'd been peeking at
her, too.

But there was a wounded warrior vibe to him, too. Some
deep sorrow that made her wonder if she ought to just leave
him alone — which took every bit of self-control she had. The

more she waited, the more she felt the urgency of a ticking countdown.

Get this man, the desert seemed to whisper on the hot, lonely nights she spent lying alone, thinking of him. *Make him yours before it's too late.*

Those words became part of a dream that visited her every night.

Too late for what?

Too late for you and for him, the voice said with a startling note of finality.

She'd wake with a shiver every time. Sometimes, a nightmare followed that dream. She was sprinting through the woods, fleeing some great evil. Then she tripped — every time, she tripped, even though she knew it was coming — and a man grabbed her. She struggled but couldn't get free, and suddenly came face-to-face with the scarred sneer of Emmett LeBlanc.

You, he cackled, pinning her down.

Sometimes it was even worse. Sometimes, Emmett wrestled her to her feet and forced her to hold a rifle to a bear's head.

Pull the trigger. Kill it. Kill it before I kill you. His face twisted in fury, and his fingers squeezed hers.

Bang! The rifle cracked through her dream, and she jolted upright with a cry.

She panted like she'd really been running and clutched the sheets.

"Anna?"

Her head snapped toward the shadow in the doorway, and a wave of relief washed over her when she realized it was Todd, checking if she was okay.

I'm okay. Fine. Thanks, she wanted to say, but all she could get out was a squeak.

Todd padded into the room and squatted down beside her. His chest was bare, his sweatpants low on his hips. He tilted his head at her, and his eyes showed the kind of pain only a man who'd experienced terrible things knew.

He sat on the bed and wrapped his thick arms around her. He tucked his chin over her head, enveloping her completely in what felt like a cloak of steel, and rocked her a little, promising nothing would get past him — no evil, real or perceived.

"I'm okay. I'm okay," she managed a minute or two later, even though she never wanted him to let go.

He didn't let go, thank goodness. Not for a long, long time, even after her breathing slowed and the sweat dried on her forehead. He kept right on holding her, and she had the distinct impression the comforting feeling wasn't a one-way thing. Had her nightmares brought back visions of his own? Had she reminded him of something he'd rather have left in the past?

"It's okay," she murmured, swaying slowly with him.

A cat screeched somewhere down the back alley, and they both turned then finally edged apart.

"You good?" He cupped her face with one big hand — the one he usually kept clenched at his side, hiding the scars — and stroked her cheek with his thumb. It was the hand that she guessed had been crushed in an accident not too long ago, but it seemed to work pretty well now that it was touching her. Not too hard, not too soft. A strong, reassuring presence, like the rest of him.

"I'm good," she whispered.

He looked at her a moment longer, then tugged her closer and kissed her on the forehead. A chaste, you'll-be-okay-now kiss. Given that the good dreams she'd had all featured him kissing her in a totally different way, she ought to have felt frustrated or sad. But somehow, that kiss was just perfect for tonight.

"Goodnight," he murmured, sliding away.

The only thing she would have changed would be to keep him curled up beside her for a few minutes. Better yet, hours.

"Goodnight," she echoed, watching him go.

His chest rose and fell in a deep breath that told her leaving was the last thing he wanted to do, and she had to wonder what was developing between them. A profound friendship or something more?

She vacillated between those options for the rest of the night, fantasizing about how good it would feel to have him touch her in so many other places. God, to be wrapped up by that body, not just his arms. To be cherished by the soul that shone so clearly in those incredible blue eyes.

Keep dreaming, Anna, she decided, looking at her disheveled hair in the mirror the next morning. The slanting dawn light highlighted every tangle, every embarrassing clump, and by the time she'd straightened it enough to appear in public, Todd's footsteps had retreated down the stairs and outside.

"Sleep well?" Sarah asked her when they bumped into each other over the coffee machine in the back room of the café.

She kept her eyes firmly on the wisps of steam rising from her mug. "Sort of. Kind of."

"Well enough for a hike later today?" Sarah's eyes sparkled.

Anna straightened, suddenly raring to go. A hike was just what she needed to take her mind off the nightmares. "God, yes. Anytime."

Sarah laughed and clinked coffee mugs with her. "It's been too long, hasn't it?"

"Way too long."

Every summer when she'd visited Montana, she and Sarah had gone hiking. Short afternoon hikes to the sparkling creek at the bend in the trail. Long, all-day treks to mountain meadows covered in wildflowers. They'd even overnighted a few times, hiking all the way up to the saddle between Cooper's Hill and Bear Mountain and pitching camp high above the tree line.

"Okay, then. It's a date. We'll go after work," Sarah promised.

Business was slow enough that they could leave shortly before noon. It was hot out, but bearable. Soren was busy in the saloon, but Jessica had offered to keep an eye on the baby while they were gone.

Sarah checked her watch. "Okay, I've got four hours until mommy duty starts again."

They headed for Anna's car, where Soren caught up to them with a worried frown.

"You're going hiking? Alone?"

"I'm not alone," Sarah said. "I'm with Anna."

"You know what I mean."

A face-off ensued, and though they both kept perfectly silent, their facial expressions shifted and changed as if they were still in full conversation. Anna looked back and forth between them, wondering if they'd already developed the telepathy some older couples did after decades together.

Finally, Soren scratched his head. "Simon and I both have to work. Cole is still out on the ranch..."

"Why do we need anyone to go with us?" Anna demanded, bristling a little at the suggestion that they couldn't handle things on their own.

Sarah and Soren exchanged pained looks.

"Janna was jumped at a bar not too long ago, and we had a break-in at the saloon," Soren said. "It's just better to be cautious, all right?"

She was about to protest, but it appeared that Soren had finished going through his mental list of escorts and finally decided on one.

"Todd," he said. "Todd can go with you."

That suggestion, Anna didn't protest.

Sarah, on the other hand, pinched her lips, and her brow folded into worried lines. Anna couldn't figure out why Sarah was so self-conscious around Todd. He was the same around her, in fact. When they finally squeezed into Anna's little hatchback and set off, she glanced in the rearview mirror and noticed Soren watching them go. He didn't look too happy, either, though it had been his idea.

What was going on?

The drive to the national forest was short and awkwardly silent, and when they parked at the trailhead, Todd immediately hemmed and hawed and moved aside.

"I won't be far behind," he said, letting them get a head start.

"Sure," Sarah said, taking Anna by the arm and hurrying ahead.

Anna looked back, but he was already hidden by a bend in the trail. "How will he know which trail we take?"

"He's a bea—" Sarah started, then caught herself with a cough. "He's a Black River mountain man. He'll stick with us, no problem."

Anna looked back dubiously but followed her cousin's lead. Before long, they were striding along the winding trail under tall stands of scented pine. The carpet of pine needles littering the ground muffled their footsteps, and the only sounds were the flutter of bird wings through the woods.

"It's beautiful," Anna murmured. Clusters of rust-colored rocks dotted clearings between rich stands of green pine, a landscape unlike any she'd ever seen. The air was crisp and clear without being painfully dry, and in the shade, the temperature was just perfect.

"In Montana, we'd be hiking through the first snow," Sarah laughed.

"Do you miss it?"

Sarah went from thoughtful to sad before brightening again. "I miss my parents. I'd give anything to go back up there and show them their grandson." Her voice cracked, and she swallowed hard. "But I have a new life now, and I love it. I really love it." Her voice practically sang. "I love discovering Arizona. I can't wait for Teddy to get bigger so we can take him on longer hikes, too."

Anna smiled. "I can totally picture Teddy looking out from a hiking backpack on Soren's back. He'd feel like the king of the mountain."

And damned if her imagination didn't conjure up its own vision: a hike with a baby of her own, carried by Todd, who wrapped his fingers around hers as they walked.

"Of course, we'll have to put off longer hikes if we have another," Sarah mused, then threw a hand over her mouth. "Oh, God. I'm sorry."

Anna forced a smile. She'd been around enough friends with babies to have received that mortified, *I-just-remembered-not-to-say-that* look. "No problem. I'm glad for you. And this way, I get to be an aunt, right?"

She told herself that would be almost as good as being a mother.

64

"Anna..." Sarah said.

She shook her head. Really, being an aunt would be great. And besides, she didn't truly have to face up to the fact that she couldn't have kids for another ten or fifteen years, when she hit forty or forty-five, right? In the meantime, she could just pretend she wasn't interested.

"Are you still in touch with Jeff?" Sarah asked.

Anna snorted at the mention of her ex-husband. "He's in touch with me. Does that count? Every year, he sends me a Christmas card with a picture of his growing flock, along with that curvy blonde he decided was worthy of bearing his children."

Yeah, her voice was bitter. But she couldn't help it. It had taken Jeff exactly thirteen months to leapfrog from her third miscarriage to hooking up with Madame Ovary and becoming a proud father — of three, by last count.

"What a jerk," Sarah muttered.

No kidding. But at least she'd found out what a louse the man was before it was too late. Yes, she wanted kids, but kids with the right kind of guy. A true partner who was steady. Loyal. Honest.

Her mind flashed through a dozen faces of men like so many images on a slot machine, and Todd popped up in the winning row every time.

"I'm glad it worked out for you and Soren," she said, trying to change the subject. "You two are made for each other."

Sarah beamed.

"And the baby looks a lot like him. That's so cute."

Sarah's face fell briefly, then went carefully neutral. "Nice view, huh?" she murmured, gesturing with one hand.

It was nice. Spectacular, really. Anna stepped closer to the overlook and took in the rocky outcrops, green mountains, and a long, winding valley that looked like the road to paradise. A dusty version of paradise, but a serene one. Anna closed her eyes, taking in the smells along with the sights, and her toes curled inside her hiking boots as if to take a bite of the earth under her feet.

"Hey, can I ask you a question?" Anna asked as they walked on.

"Sure."

"How well do you know Todd?" She nearly winced at the obvious interest in her voice.

Sarah studied her. "He's a great guy."

Anna wondered why her cousin looked so pained.

"A really great guy. A lot like Soren." Sarah looked away and bit her lip. She took a sip of water from Anna's bottle before continuing. "You like him, don't you?"

Anna couldn't stop an instinctive *Who, me?* expression from taking over her face. But who was she kidding? Yes, she liked Todd. She'd been spending days and nights dreaming about the man. Wondering if she was right to hold back or whether she ought to make a move.

"Look, Anna," Sarah started. Her voice was low and hesitant. "I have to talk to you."

Anna took a sip of water from her bottle, preparing herself to hear about whatever it was that haunted Todd so much. He was out of earshot, and though she didn't like talking about people behind their backs, it might help her understand him better.

Sarah hemmed and hawed for a while, and Anna watched her out of the corner of her eye. Sarah, the lucky thing, had grown up as Todd's neighbor. She'd spent so much time with Soren, she had to have known Todd, too. So why the shyness, the beating around the bush?

"You remember when Soren and I broke up for a while?"

Anna nodded, remembering the teary phone calls. She'd reassured Sarah as much as she could because she knew it would somehow work out. And it had.

"I guess Soren asked Todd to keep an eye on me when he was gone..."

Anna chuckled. "A little like now?"

Sarah's smile was thin, her face strained. "I guess. Anyway, I got to know Todd pretty well."

Anna listened eagerly for her cousin to say something like, *He's perfect for you!*

"But... well..."

What? Anna wanted to shake the words out of her. What?

"Todd is Teddy's f—"

Whatever Sarah was trying to say got cut off by a short, sharp bark. Something between a howl and a snarl. They both stepped back, scanning the hill to their left.

"What was that?" Sarah cried, pulling on Anna's arm.

Something moved behind the trees, and a pair of bloodshot eyes flashed at them through the leaves.

Anna's blood ran cold. "Is that a wolf?"

Sarah clutched her arm. "Back up slowly. Stay close."

They'd had their share of animal encounters in the past, but something about this beast seemed different. The eyes that darted between the two of them were the eyes of a predator, not an animal caught by surprise. It lowered its muzzle and stepped forward, snarling openly.

Anna had never had a wild animal approach her. Most fled the second they spotted humans. The bears she and Sarah had occasionally seen in Montana had quickly turned away, disinterested, and even the bobcat they'd once stumbled across had quickly decided to retreat.

This animal, though, stalked forward, one deliberate step at a time, showing its fangs.

"Maybe just a coyote?" she asked out of the corner of her mouth.

"Wolf," Sarah murmured, her voice full of dread.

Anna didn't know there were wolves in Arizona, let alone big, nasty ones. She hooked elbows with Sarah and leaned down to pick up a stick. For now, she kept it at her side, but if the wolf came any closer, she'd brandish it and yell. That always worked, right?

The wolf stepped closer, snarling, and a stream of saliva dripped from the corner of its mouth.

"Is it rabid?" she whispered.

Sarah's body was stiff and tense. "Not rabid. Something worse."

What was worse than rabid? Anna didn't want to find out. She raised her stick and opened her mouth to shout.

What came out, though, wasn't just a shout. It was a roar. By the time she realized it wasn't coming from her, she was sprawling across the ground. Sarah pushed her into a dive as a massive shape barreled out of the woods behind them and made for the wolf.

Anna rolled, and everything blurred. Then her knee knocked into a rock, and Sarah grunted beside her.

Todd. Her first thought was that Todd had raced up to chase the wolf away. But since when did Todd — quiet, reserved Todd — roar like a lion and tackle wild animals with his bare hands?

"Come on! Run!" Sarah urged, pulling her up.

They sprinted back down the path. Anna threw a glance over her shoulder but couldn't see anything amidst the trail of shaking branches left in the wake of whatever had chased down the wolf. Both had raced out of sight behind the ridgeline, but another roar sounded, along with a ferocious canine snarl.

"Jesus, what was that?"

"A wolf," Sarah said, taking huge, leaping bounds.

"No, I mean... I didn't see what chased it away. Was that Todd?" The more she thought about it, the more she was sure it couldn't have been him. It felt like him, somehow, but hadn't she seen a powerful, furry animal streak past on four feet?

"It was Todd," Sarah said in a strangely certain voice.

Anna halted in her tracks. "We have to go help him. We can't leave him alone."

Sarah looked back. The woods had gone eerily quiet. No growls, no roars. Not even a bird call. It was as if the whole forest was holding its breath, wondering if the danger had passed.

"Believe me, he'll be okay. We should get out of here, though."

"But—"

Sarah pulled her downhill at a more careful trot. "I'm still new to all this, but I think we'd better get home."

New to all what? Anna looked at her cousin. Sarah knew all about wilderness and animals and safety in the woods. She'd grown up with the Rockies as her backyard. Maybe Sarah meant she was new to rabid creatures attacking her out of nowhere? Well, that was a first for Anna, too.

"Are you sure Todd will be okay?" she asked. Her heart pumped madly, and every nerve in her body was on high alert.

Sarah reassured her all the way back to the trailhead parking lot, where they waited by the car. They scanned the edge of the woods, ready to jump into the car at the first sign of danger. A torturously slow twenty minutes ticked by before the lengthening shadows flickered, and Todd stepped out of the woods.

His hands were dirty, as if he'd been scrambling on all fours, and a leaf stuck out of his hair. His jeans and shirt, however, were unmarred. Not a drop of sweat, not a thread torn loose.

"Todd." Anna held her breath, looking at him.

His eyes traveled up and down her body just the way hers studied him, checking for injuries. He was the one who'd gone after a wolf, for goodness sake!

"Did you see the wolf?" she couldn't help asking.

Todd didn't always hear everything, she knew, but his silence seemed deliberate this time.

Finally, he nodded as if satisfied that she was all right and exchanged a long, worried look with Sarah. The kind of look that had been bugging Anna all week because it made her feel like she was the one who couldn't hear.

"It was a wolf, wasn't it?" she asked.

Todd nodded slowly, looking right into her eyes. "Yeah, it was a wolf, all right."

"What did it do when it saw you?"

He cracked into the first cocky grin she'd ever seen on his modest face.

"He ran. Believe me, he ran."

Chapter Seven

Todd stretched his feet out as far as they would go under the dash of Soren's truck. Miles of highway stretched out before them, and although it was late afternoon, he could feel the temperature rise with every foot of their gradual descent.

"In town, we're up at five thousand feet," Soren said. "The ranch is down at four thousand, but it's still bearable there. It's when you drop way down to Phoenix that things really heat up."

Todd watched Soren talk, trying to match the motion of his lips to the words his cousin shot into his mind. It didn't seem like he'd get his hearing back anytime soon, so he might as well figure out lip-reading, just in case. That, or he could just hang around bears for the rest of his life. Bears and Anna, because everything she said, he heard.

Because she's my mate. His bear nodded, all matter-of-fact.

If only it were that simple.

Soren stuck a finger out over the steering wheel. "There it is. Twin Moon Ranch."

Todd caught a glimpse of a few rooftops way, way out in the middle of nowhere off the west side of the road. One second, he saw them, and the next, they were gone. Which, he supposed, suited the wolf pack perfectly. All shifters were secretive, keeping a low profile from prying human eyes. Soren and his unusual little bear-wolf clan were among the few who lived right in the middle of a town.

Todd closed his eyes and inhaled deeply, thinking of home. He could see what Soren liked about Arizona, but dang, there was only one home for him. Montana.

Anna would like it there, his bear murmured.

Yeah, he'd bet she would. But his bear had to quit thinking along those lines.

She's our mate. How can we possibly keep away?

His bear just didn't get it. Montana was exactly where the Blue Blood rogues had made their boldest attack, wiping out most of his clan in an ambush that had also targeted the neighboring wolf pack and Anna's family, all due to a crazy belief that shifters shouldn't cross species lines. How could he bring his mate to Montana if he couldn't keep her safe there?

Soren said the Blue Bloods were finished. He, Sarah, and the Twin Moon wolves wiped them out.

Todd didn't answer. How could he really be sure? Purist groups like the Blue Bloods were like the snakes of Hydra's head — if you cut one off, three more grew back. Who knew whether the wolf shifter he'd chased off was one of the Blue Bloods or not?

The second Soren heard about their encounter, he'd packed Todd into his truck and headed for Twin Moon Ranch, leaving Simon and the others to run the saloon. They sped down the highway until Soren took an unmarked turn onto a dirt lane that didn't appear to lead anywhere. But it wound on for a full three miles of scrubby desert — a solid buffer to the outside world — before curving right and crossing a bridge over a dry creek bed.

Todd shook his head. God, did he miss the rushing rivers and cool mountain streams of home.

The truck rattled under a wide gateway, and Todd ducked for a better look at the ranch brand that hung from it. Two circles, overlapping by a third.

"Twin Moon Ranch." Soren nodded, seeing him look. "One of the most powerful wolf packs in the Southwest." He tipped his head from side to side. "Maybe *the* most powerful pack."

The place looked like a tiny frontier town, with rows of false-front buildings on two sides. Giant cottonwoods sheltered a central square, and a smattering of houses extended all around. Beyond them lay pastures full of brown quarter horses and spotted cows, all quietly flicking their tails in the slanting afternoon light.

The wolf pack alpha eyed their approach from the porch of a slope-roofed building on the right.

"That's Ty Hawthorne," Soren murmured.

Typical wolf: not quite as broad as a bear, but sturdy and plenty tall. Todd could feel the power concentrated in the man's laser gaze. The brunette at the alpha's side was almost as tall and lanky, except for a visible baby bump. Unlike the dead-serious alpha, she looked friendly, even welcoming.

"Hi. Welcome to the ranch," she called out as he and Soren approached.

Hi, and watch you don't cross me, her mate's thunderous expression said.

Alphas were always a bit gruff, and they got fiercely protective around their mates. And if this alpha's mate was pregnant... Well, Todd knew to watch out, just in case.

He expected the wolf alpha to wait on the porch. It was a hierarchy thing, and no one was bigger on hierarchy than wolves. But the man shocked the hell out of him by descending the stairs — all four of them, all the way to the ground — to greet Soren with a hearty handshake. The two looked at each other for a long, quiet minute, just like Todd remembered his grandfather doing with the leader of the local wolf pack at home. A meeting of equals.

He stared at his cousin. He always knew Soren would become a respected alpha someday, but to see him actually accomplish that... Well, if Todd had been wearing a hat, he'd have doffed it to his cousin.

Way to go, man. He wanted to whistle. *Way to go.*

Soren's lips moved as he gestured, and Todd saw Ty Hawthorne's eyes jump to him. The wolf shifter's lips moved, too, and Todd tipped his head, trying to catch the words.

Nothing. Not a thing. He'd heard the she-wolf pretty clearly, but the alpha? No chance. All he caught was a faint scratch from far, far away.

Ty Hawthorne narrowed his eyes and spoke again, starting to look angry. But then the she-wolf stepped forward, bumped the alpha's arm, and said something that looked like, *He can't hear you, dummy.*

Todd hid a grin. That woman was definitely the alpha's mate, and it was pretty clear the power she wielded.

"Does this work?" she asked, speaking and thinking the words at the same time. "I'm Lana."

Todd nodded. "Yeah, that works. Thanks."

Most shifters couldn't read each other's thoughts unless they were relatives or packmates. But powerful shifters could if they opened their minds to each other and tried hard enough. And to his credit, Ty Hawthorne tried. His brow furrowed and his eyes flashed, but that time, Todd heard him.

"Come inside. Tell me about the wolf you saw."

Soren pursed his lips in a gesture that said, *I told you he's the straight-to-business type.* Which was a case of the pot calling the kettle black, for sure, though Todd decided not to say that.

They filed into the cool shade of the building in strict order of rank — first the she-wolf, then her mate, then Soren, and finally Todd.

Yeah, he got the message. He was the outsider here, the unknown bear. Even so, he stretched tall and made sure he met Ty Hawthorne's eyes straight on in a not-so-subtle message of his own. He might not be a clan alpha, but he was powerful in his own right.

It wasn't until a minute later that he realized he wasn't powerful anymore, not with all his injuries. Still, Ty looked him up and down then gave a curt nod.

I'll give you a chance, bear, that nod said. *Exactly one.*

Another two wolves were standing in the room, and one offered a friendly handshake.

"Hiya. I'm Cody," said an easygoing blond guy. He followed Lana's lead and shot his thoughts across along with the words spilling from his lips.

Cody Hawthorne. Ty's brother, Soren whispered in an aside aimed exclusively at Todd. *Ty takes care of the big issues, and Cody keeps on eye on the day-to-day stuff.*

Todd didn't have to work hard to figure out which of the two brothers had the people skills and which had the raw power.

"Nice to meet you. I'm Tina," said a dark-haired beauty who looked a lot like Ty.

The sister. She runs the neighboring ranch with her mate, Soren said.

Todd shook her hand, hiding his amazement. The wolf pack spread across not one, but two huge ranches? No wonder they were a force to be reckoned with.

He looked from one face to another. Were they a force powerful enough to stamp out the Blue Bloods?

"Tell me what happened," Ty barked.

Soren explained what Sarah had described to him. The problem was, Sarah was a human who'd only been turned bear shifter recently when she mated with Soren. She didn't have the experience to differentiate subtleties between shifters yet.

Todd nodded along. When Sarah and Anna had set off on their hike, he'd stripped and shifted to follow them in bear form. He hadn't shifted in days, and his body had ached for the chance. And man, did it feel good — really good — to sniff and roll and claw a few trees. Even his damaged foot did okay, so the limping wasn't too bad, and he could easily keep up. So he'd let the women get ahead of him at one point, figuring he could catch up. The second the wolf howled, he'd barreled upslope so fast, the trees became a blur.

No one threatens my mate! his bear had bellowed. *No one!*

In his rush to intercept the wolf, he'd dashed right past Anna, who Sarah had shoved into a dive. In part, he figured, to get her out of the way, and in part to prevent her from getting a good look at him in bear form.

I want her to see me, his bear grumbled inside. *To accept me. To love me.*

Well, Todd wanted that, too, but that had hardly been the time.

When, then? his bear demanded.

He hung his head. Maybe never.

"Todd." Soren's voice boomed into his mind, and he looked up.

Oops. Everyone was looking at him, expecting the answer to a question he'd missed.

"Can you describe the wolf?" Lana asked gently — and quickly, he figured, before Ty did something like smack him over the head.

"You're sure it was a shifter?" Tina added, helping him along.

He nodded. Even Sarah knew it was a shifter. She just didn't recognize which one.

"It definitely wasn't one of the Black River wolves from Jess and Janna's pack. And not any of the Blue Bloods involved in the ambush."

Normally, a single rogue wolf might not have aroused so much concern. But everyone had learned not to underestimate the Blue Bloods.

"I was hoping we got the last of them," Tina Hawthorne sighed.

"Maybe we did," Ty snarled, but even he didn't sound entirely convinced.

The leaders had been eliminated, but there was no telling whether the movement had been stamped out or whether it had only gone underground.

"You're sure it wasn't one of the Blue Bloods?" Cody asked.

Todd gritted his teeth and searched memories he'd have preferred not to explore too closely. He'd barely managed to get Sarah out of the burning house in Black River when the Blue Blood wolves had come swarming at him. He'd pushed her toward his truck and stood guard while she got away, then fought like the warrior he'd been raised to be. But one bear was no match for twenty wolves, and they'd wrestled him to the ground. Some stayed in wolf form, while others shifted to human shape and battered his body with bricks and bats, howling at him the entire time. He could feel one rogue stomp on his hand and pin it against a rock while another smashed it again and again, shattering every bone, tearing every sinew.

Purity. Purity. Their triumphant cries echoed in his mind, louder and more clearly than any sound he'd caught in the past couple of months. He just about jammed his hands over his ears, but then another memory jumped out of nowhere and sang to him in a melody he strained to hear.

Stay with me. Don't die. Not now. Not like this.

Wait a minute. He knew that voice.

Think of mountain meadows in spring. Thick of a clear, cool summer creek...

Anna. The woman who'd talked him out of dying was Anna?

Think of berries growing thick in the fall...

It was as if she'd looked into his mind, discovered all his favorite things, and written them all into a poem just for him.

Anna had been there at the beginning of this mess. And Jesus, Anna was the one who'd facilitated his escape from the cage he'd been kept in at the wildlife center.

But, wait a minute. Wasn't he mad at her for tricking him into staying alive when he should have died? If it weren't for her, he would have died a hero, and none of the suffering he'd endured since then would have happened.

But none of the good moments would have happened, either, he realized. Like meeting her in the park the day he thought his head would split. Like seeing her smile. Like getting to hold her after her nightmare.

How can I be mad at my mate? his bear grumbled. *It wasn't her fault. It's fate.*

He blinked a few times, trying to make sense of it. Wait. Maybe fate hadn't been screwing with him. Maybe fate had given him a choice.

Die a hero, or live on and hold out for your mate.

His hands shook, because he knew what that meant. Fate never negotiated and it never offered choices — except in the rarest circumstances.

The truest heroes, the ones who serve most loyally — those who put others above their own good — sometimes, fate rewards them with something it doesn't give anyone else. He remembered his great-grandfather's ancient voice scratching out the words. He remembered it perfectly, right down to the gestures of the old man's leathery hands and the crackle of wood in the fireplace on that winter's night, a long time ago.

Fate gives them a choice, his great-grandfather had said. *A choice that risks more suffering, but gives them the possibility of an even greater end. Their own destiny. One they fight for, if they're brave enough to try.*

His hands shook, and he gulped for air. Jesus, how could that possibly be him?

He wanted to grab Soren and ask him if he remembered that story, too. He wanted to race back in time and study his own actions, because he hadn't been trying to be a hero. He'd just done what he had to do.

But everyone was staring at him now, so he rocked back on his heels and gulped. He could have cut through the tension in the room with his pinkie claw if he could coordinate himself to move just then.

Lucky thing Tina stepped forward, cutting the tension a different way.

"Such a hot day," she murmured, handing him a glass. "How about a drink, everyone?"

She pressed something cool and moist into his hand — his good hand, bless her, so the chances of him dropping it were low.

"Lemonade," she said casually, settling his nerves. "My Aunt Jean made it, and it's really good."

It was a cue for him to drink, and he obeyed. She even stood in front of him while he brought the glass to his mouth, helping hide the shake in his hand and the pale hue he felt come over his face.

Tina passed glasses around to the others, and it was all so smooth, so natural. Not so much a cover-up as a friendly little break.

Thanks, he murmured, directing the thought to Tina's mind and no one else.

Tina winked.

I know something about big bad alphas needing a helping hand from time to time.

He smiled then froze. Wait a second. He wasn't an alpha. He was just...

Tina shook her head at him, sending an audible *tsk-tsk* into his mind.

Obviously, the she-wolf didn't know him as well as she thought, but now was hardly the time to push that point.

"So, it wasn't one of the Blue Bloods," Cody said, picking up the conversation where he'd left off.

"At least, not one directly involved in the attacks."

"Maybe we got all of them," Cody said, looking hopeful if not certain.

Ty shook his head. "Hard to say. But they might as well be out there, the way shifters all over the West are panicking."

Just when Todd was about to ask what that meant, Lana supplied the answer.

"Mixed shifter couples living in outlying places have been contacting us, looking for a safer place. Looking to band together. There are rumors of new attacks, but so far, none we can prove. No one knows if the Blue Bloods are still out there or not."

Ty shook his head and rapped his knuckles on a table, calling the conversation back to the main point. "Where exactly did this wolf show up?"

Todd cast his mind back to the previous day's hike, because that was easier to handle than the distant past. "I think it's called Sunrise Trail. It went up like this..." He drew the landscape with his hands, and the others nodded along. "There was a hollow, then a rise, and then a little ridge you don't see from below."

"I know the spot." Ty nodded. "Good place to surprise someone."

"You got any rogues around here I don't know about?" Soren curved an eyebrow, and Todd could see the anger in his cousin's tight lips.

Ty shook his head firmly, but the gesture slowly stalled out. "Nono. Unless..."

"Unless?" Soren demanded.

Ty, Tina, and Cody exchanged glances, and Todd caught the whisper of a name.

"Roy."

"Who the hell is Roy?" Soren demanded.

Tina opened her hands in the air, a signal for the bear to cool down. Her face had gone from thoughtful to sad. "A member of our pack."

"A rogue member of your pack?" Soren barked, enraged at the idea that his mate had been threatened by one of his allies.

The Twin Moon wolves shook their heads. "He's not a rogue," Tina said quickly. "It's just that... Well..."

Cody continued where she left off. "We grew up together. He's a good guy. But after... Well, after a tragedy—" Cody said, glossing over the details "—he started staying in wolf form for longer and longer periods of time."

A hush fell over the room.

"How long has he been in wolf form?" Soren asked.

Cody looked at Ty, who looked at Tina.

"How long?" Soren demanded.

Tina gave a sad sigh. "Six years."

Soren shot Todd a look that said, *holy crap.* Wolf shifters were like bears in that their human sides were dominant. To stay in animal form too long meant risking one's sanity, as Todd knew all too well. He'd stayed in bear form for months, and he'd felt the strands of sanity unravel, one thin thread at a time. Who knows what might have happened if he'd remained a bear for longer?

And six years... Holy crap was right.

Ty ran a hand through his hair. "Roy wouldn't hurt anyone — I think."

"Let's not jump to conclusions," Tina said. "It could have been an outsider who wandered onto our territory."

"Well, I want him out. Yesterday," Ty barked.

"We'll send our best trackers out," Cody said.

Ty nodded. "Put Zack on it. And Kyle."

"And I'll rustle up our best hands to help keep an eye on things in town," Tina said. "We let them slack off a bit since the last attack. Maybe that was a mistake."

Soren growled under his breath, and Todd understood his frustration. On the one hand, Soren's pride demanded that he protect his clan with his own resources. On the other hand, he was ready to go to any length to protect those he loved.

Yeah, Todd got that part. He got it very well.

Part of his mind had still been teasing apart the concept of fate giving him a choice. But now, he shoved all that aside. It wasn't time to think. It was time to act. To protect.

Soren caught his eye and gave him a dark look. *I know it's hard for you to stay, but I need you, man. Will you stay until we're sure it's safe for everyone?*

Soren meant Sarah, Teddy, and the other members of his clan, but front and foremost among them, Todd saw an image of Anna.

Will you do it? Soren repeated.

Did he have to ask?

I'm with you, he nodded. *Whatever it takes.*

Chapter Eight

That night, Anna's dreams were haunted by diabolical wolves, and she very nearly cried out for Todd again. She only managed to coax herself back to bed by thinking of better things — like Todd holding her. Kissing her. Touching her. Whispering her name.

In the dreams that followed the nightmares, her mind played out a thousand sultry encounters. But by the time she got up in the morning to help Jessica bake, Todd was already gone.

"Damn it." She scowled into the mirror and forced herself to get moving.

But he'd forgotten something, apparently, because he came back up the stairs when she headed out, and just like that, her mood lifted again.

"Morning," he murmured, stopping with one foot on her step and one foot on the step below. That put them eye to eye, and she lost her breath. From so close up, she could make out the pattern of his irises, where lighter blues intersected with darker indigo like so many panes of stained glass.

"Morning," she whispered.

Taking a deep breath had been a mistake because he smelled so good. She wanted to nuzzle her chin up and down his jaw. She wanted to tuck her cheek against his chest. To run her hands up and down his arms.

And oops, she really did reach out for his arm.

His lips moved, and his eyes dropped to her mouth. His chest rose and fell with every breath, and hers did, too, in perfect time with him.

Kiss him. Kiss him. A chant started up in her head.

He tilted his head a tiny bit, and God, that brought him to the perfect angle for a brush of the lips.

Kiss him. Kiss him.

It was just like that time in sixth grade when she'd been all the way up the high dive board at the community pool, and all the kids had egged her on from below.

Go. Go. Go.

Her hands tightened on his shirt — somewhere along the line, her fingers seemed to have snuck over to his chest — and she held her breath.

He was so close. So quiet. So focused on her.

It was impossible *not* to kiss him. Even the songbirds outside seemed to cheer her on.

Kiss me, his eyes begged.

So she did. She tilted her chin up, closed her eyes, and leaned in for a kiss. And the second their lips met...

She'd been expecting fireworks, but it felt more like slipping into a warm bath on a cold day. The kind that commanded you to sigh with pleasure and let every single muscle relax. His lips covered hers and moved slightly, as if he were whispering while kissing — and maybe he was. Not that she could hear anything over the swoosh of her pulse in her ears.

After one soft kiss, they eased apart. But just as gently, they leaned back in for another. And another and another, until his hand slid behind her neck and tugged her closer. Her fingers knotted tightly in his shirt, and her breath came as quickly as if she'd been running up the stairs instead of standing still, and—

"Anna!" Jessica called from below. "Are you ready to give me a hand?"

They both whipped around, holding their breath. Why, she couldn't tell. The kiss felt so right — light-years from wrong. So why the jolt? Why let all that space come between them when close felt so much better?

Todd gulped and closed his eyes, and she did, too, hanging on to the memory of what had just transpired.

"I have to go," she whispered.

He caught a lock of her hair in one finger and twirled it around, then smiled as if some great secret had been revealed to him.

"Been wanting to do that for a long time," he confessed.

Been wanting you to do that for a long time, she nearly said.

One second, he was grinning, and the next, all mournful. And then he was gone.

He was busy all day, damn it, and so was she. And yet, a second didn't tick by without her thinking of him. Every time she greeted a new customer, she wished it was him. Every time she served a drink, she imagined bringing Todd one that was colder and bigger. And every time the clock ticked, she wondered when she might get the chance to see him again.

To kiss him again, her subconscious added hopefully.

"I feel bad. You're supposed to be visiting, not working your butt off," Sarah said when Anna bustled into the saloon after helping close down the café for the afternoon.

"Really, I'm happy to help," she said, wiping down a table.

"I like Anna working her butt off," Janna added with a grin. "I've gotten to sleep in every morning this week."

Anna laughed. "All of you work so hard. I can't believe you manage so many back-to-back shifts."

It was true. Everyone worked hard to make the café and the saloon a success, and she was happy to be part of it in some way. At her real estate office in Virginia, there was never a feeling of a common goal the way there was here.

"Now you're the one doing back-to-back shifts," Sarah pointed out.

Anna shrugged. "I like being busy, and I like getting to know everyone here."

Like Todd? the back of her mind chipped in before slipping into daydreams again.

Yes, Todd. She was dying to see him again. The one time she'd managed to make an excuse to bring him a drink, Soren had been around, so she couldn't throw herself into another kiss. Still, it lit up her soul just to see him.

It was pathetic, how excited she got about little moments like those. The sight of his eyes lighting up when he saw her, and the way he held her gaze when he brought the coffee mug to his lips. Lips she spent way, way too much time thinking about.

Hours ticked by, and the whole time, she wondered when she might see him again.

"Hey," Janna said at ten p.m. "I can handle the rest. You can call it a night."

Anna looked around. "You sure?"

There were still a good two dozen customers in the saloon, most of them German tourists who were glued to a soccer game they'd begged Simon to tune the TV to. A team in red with far too many consonants in its name was tied with a team in white, and everyone was very excited about who might win.

"No problem. They've all eaten, so it'll only be drinks from now on. Thanks again." Janna waved her toward the back door.

Anna hung her apron in the kitchen and emptied her tips into the tip jar everyone shared. Then she walked out through the back room, stopping to admire the bar Todd had been restoring. Soren had been excited to discover a beautiful rosewood pattern inlaid around the edge, and she ran a finger along the diamond-in-a-square design, leading all the way down the serving counter like a tiny railroad track. God, it was going to be beautiful. Hell, it was already beautiful. Todd had toiled over every hard edge, every impossible-to-reach corner, every delicate curve. Other than a stack of used sandpaper in the corner, he'd left everything neat as a pin, ready for work the next day.

She nodded in respect. Todd was leaving his mark on this special place.

She looked at it for another minute, wondering what mark she might leave. Not sure if she liked the word *leave* at all.

So, Sarah, I was wondering. . .

The speech she'd been toying with raced through her mind. But once again, she batted down the urge to find Sarah and ask if she could stay longer. Stay forever, possibly — or at least as long as Todd did, which seemed as up in the air as her own plans. But she'd stretched her visit out to two weeks already, and while Sarah had been welcoming, she hadn't actually invited Anna to move in.

Unfortunately.

Walking out the back door, she stepped into the cool night air and tilted her head up to the indigo sky.

"Wow," she murmured aloud.

There looked to be about a million stars out in that perfectly clear Arizona sky. The moon was nowhere to be seen, and the Milky Way could have been a speckled highway, it was that distinct and bright. She'd only ever seen it stand out so bold and bright one other time, and that had been one summer in Montana, a long time ago.

Montana. . . Arizona. Her mind bounced from one to the other. She'd never felt as at peace as she did in two places she'd never been able to call home.

She took a few steps forward and craned her neck for a better view. What she really needed was a meadow to lie in, just like she'd done that summer way back when.

Then it occurred to her that while she might not have a meadow, she did have the next best thing. Todd had started work on the deck upstairs, and she'd bet the stars looked even brighter from up there. In fact, hadn't Janna asked Todd to carry up the roll of unused Astroturf they'd found among all the odds and ends in the garage?

Come on, then. Come on up, the stars seemed to call, all of them twinkling as one.

There were two ways up to the deck: through a door from the apartment over the saloon or up a set of fire stairs that started in the rear lot. She took the latter and ascended slowly, watching the stars as she went.

The deck had been built over the flat roof of a room that had been added on to the saloon years ago, and it played a central role in the grand plans everyone had for the apartment upstairs.

"We can barbecue there!" Janna had clapped when she came up with the idea.

"Maybe put in a little baby pool." Sarah had sighed.

"With an awning," Jessica had added. "A place we can chill out and relax since we don't really have a yard."

Of course, the deck was a work in progress, like the rest of the apartment. The last time she'd taken a peek, it was just a sloppily tarred surface with a couple of provisional safety rails.

A flash made her snap her head up just as she reached the level of the deck. A shooting star?

"Make a wish," Todd called softly.

She whipped around in surprise, her heart already skipping joyfully.

He was lying on his back with his hands behind his head, studying the stars. Or was he studying her?

She glanced at him just in time to catch his eyes sliding back to the sky.

Hurry up and make your wish, the crickets seemed to call.

She closed her eyes and pictured a replay of their kiss.

"Got it?" Todd asked.

She nodded slowly. Yeah, she'd made her wish. The question was, would it come true? Watching Todd lie there, more relaxed than she'd ever seen him, made her wish even more.

"Wow. This is great," she said, stepping onto the deck and looking around. The rough surface was gone, hidden under a layer of wood. A carpet of Astroturf was spread over the middle like a patch of grass. In the moonlight, it could have passed for the real thing, soft and springy under her feet.

"Not quite a mountain meadow, but it will do," Todd murmured.

She tilted her head at him. Was the man a mind reader, or were they both wired the same way?

She motioned to the space beside him. "Mind if I join you?"

"Sure." His voice didn't sound as relaxed as his posture.

She sat beside him, suddenly self-conscious, and slipped her sandals off to test the lawn with her toes.

Todd studied her. "What do you think?"

She glanced at his bare feet. The two of them really were wired the same way.

"Well. . ." She wiggled her toes. "It's better than it was. Way better."

He chuckled a little but went quiet the second she stretched out beside him. Not too close, but not too far. Still, every nerve ending in her body tingled.

"Did you make a wish?" she asked after a quiet minute ticked by. Did big, quiet mountain men even make wishes?

He nodded but didn't say a thing, and she wondered what his wish had been.

She pushed her shoulders back and looked up. "God, look at the Big Dipper." She could practically see it scoop stardust out of the desert sky.

"The Great Bear," he corrected.

She angled her head this way and that. "I could never really see the bear in it. All the constellations are like that. Have you seen Taurus? It looks nothing like a bull."

"Sure it does," he said, pointing to the right.

She found it easily, but not the bull part. "It just looks like a sideways V."

He opened his hand, fingers together, thumb pointing down, and traced the shape with his other hand. The one that was all scarred up. "He's looking sideways. There's his nose, his horns." He pointed at his hand, then at the sky. "The bright one is his eye."

His. Funny how he described that constellation the way he might describe an old friend.

"Oh! I see it!" She pointed. "Hey, it really does look like a bull."

"Yep."

All the astronomy books she'd ever read drew stiff, color-by-numbers kind of lines between stars — that, or they drew impossibly swirly, intricate sketches of what the constellations were supposed to be. What they really needed were pictures of Todd's hands.

He balled them into fists and dropped them quickly out of sight, but she reached over and put them right back. So what if they were scarred? So what if the fingers of the right hand couldn't straighten all the way? Tonight, those hands were artists. Astronomers. Magicians.

"Show me another one," she asked.

His hands wavered for a second before he pointed again. "Cassiopeia."

She groaned. "That one's impossible."

"Picture a woman leaning back."

She snorted. "I see a W. Did she trip over a rock or something?"

His laugh was music to her ears. "I don't think so. But with Greek myths, you never know."

"I don't see anything like a woman."

"She's there. Look, like you." He rolled on his side and motioned toward her body. "Bend your knees a little bit."

She drew them up, squinting at the stars.

"Now lean on your elbows..."

She drew them up and laughed. "Now I look like a woman trying to pick guys up on the beach. All I need is a bikini."

He chuckled. "Maybe the Greeks left that part out of the myth. But look." He pointed up. "Cassiopeia."

She stretched back out, feeling self-conscious about the way she'd stuck her chest out. But when she refocused on the stars, she saw a woman take shape.

"Whoa. Wait. I see her."

Now she was the one talking about constellations like they were people she knew.

"See? Easy. Now the bear..." Todd emphasized the last word as if introducing the main event.

"The Dipper."

"The Bear," he insisted.

"Where?"

"The end of the dipper is his nose. He's looking left, toward his mate."

"He has a mate?"

Todd answered slowly. "Well, maybe he's looking for her."

Her heart fluttered a little at the idea. If only she could be a bear.

"The dipper is his nose," Todd repeated. Typical male —
dropping the romantic part like a hot coal. "The cup part
of the dipper is his back. Picture him wearing a little saddle
blanket or a jacket, like he's been forced to work for a circus."

His words dripped scorn, and she looked at him. Man, he
really took this bear stuff personally.

"Like that part?" When she pointed, her hand brushed his.

"Yeah. And his tail is over there, but those stars are fainter.
Mainly, you have to picture the chest part."

He motioned toward his body, and yeah, that part was easy
to equate to a bear. He was that big, that broad, that solid.

She turned away and puffed a little air toward her face.
Suddenly, she felt flush. Maybe she should concentrate on the
stars. She found the bear's nose again, followed the line of
stars along its back and—

"Oh! I see it! It's like a polar bear."

"Grizzly," he growled.

She squinted again. "How can you tell?"

"Definitely a grizzly," he said vaguely.

"Cool. I can see the bear."

"Like I said. Easy."

"You make it easy," she said. A little like falling in love
with him. Far, far too easy.

They lay in silence, looking at the stars. She found Taurus
and Cassiopeia again, just for practice, then turned back to
the bear and contemplated what Todd had said.

"Does he ever find her?" she asked.

"Find who?"

"His mate. Does he find her?"

She'd expected him to laugh, but Todd fell silent. Gravely
silent. He didn't answer for a long time.

"I'm not sure." His voice was a whisper.

She listened to the crickets chirp for a minute, wondering
why he sounded so sad.

"How does he know it's his mate?" she ventured. Was that
part of the myth, too?

Todd took a deep breath. "He knows the second he sees
her. That's the easy part."

ANNA LOWE

Huh. "So what's the hard part?" It seemed easy to her. Boy bear sees girl bear. Grunts. Growls. They get together, make adorable cubs, and—

"Making sure he's worthy of her."

She sighed. Yeah, she would definitely like to be a bear.

"I bet he is," she said, because Todd sounded a little unsure. "Look at him."

"Yeah, look at him." His voice was a little bitter, so she caught his hand and massaged it a little bit. Were they still talking about bears?

"Hey," she whispered, rolling on her side.

He looked up at the stars, not meeting her eyes.

"If the boy bear recognizes his mate the second he sees her, she's bound to recognize him, too."

His chest went up and down with a deep breath. "I'm not sure."

She snorted and leaned closer. "Before I get mad at you for implying that females are too stupid to recognize what males see right away—"

His hands flew up in protest, but she continued before he could speak.

"—let me prove to you they're not."

And she kissed him.

She had no idea what had come over her. Maybe she'd blame it on the stars and their cheery, hopeful light. Maybe it was Todd with all that talk of mates. Or maybe it was that insistent voice in the back of her mind.

Get this man. Make him yours before you miss your chance.

Whatever it was, she couldn't hold back any more. She needed that kiss.

She kissed him lightly, rolling her lips as if to stir the taste out of him. And damn, did he taste good. All male, all musky. His lips were rough around the edges but soft in the middle, and they danced slowly over hers.

She rolled closer, cupping his face and kissing deeper. Soon, not only were their lips touching but their bodies, too. Her chest squeezed against his, her legs found the perfect angle to nestle close to his, and her hips. . .

Her hips followed their own agenda, sneaking closer and closer to him.

"Anna," he whispered.

She went from kissing to nuzzling him with her chin, her cheek, her nose.

"You don't want this?"

She managed to sound confident because his body all but screamed to hers, which meant he wanted this, too. His hands cupped her waist, his legs shifted to make space for hers, and his chest rose and fell heavily.

"I want this. But—"

"No buts. Please."

"Anna—"

"You really want me to stop?" She panted beside his ear.

"I never want you to stop," he whispered.

"Then forget about everything else."

She sure had forgotten. She'd tuned out the voices drifting up from the saloon and stopped measuring the distance to the room where Sarah slept with Teddy in case one of them overheard. She quit thinking about tomorrow or what other people might think and focused entirely on the moment. Everything disappeared except for him. Her.

Him *and* her, like one thing. Their hearts beat in tandem. Their chests rose and fell at exactly the same time. And the need around them grew like a physical thing.

She slid until she wasn't just lying alongside him but *on* him, and the fire that had been crackling quietly inside her suddenly flared into a blaze. She straddled him and dragged her hips over his.

"Anna..." He wasn't protesting any more. He was urging her on.

She slid up his body then down, seeking out just the right spot.

"You know what Sarah once told me?" she asked, nibbling on his ear.

His hands slid along her ribs until they found the outline of her bra. "What did Sarah once tell you?"

93

His voice was flat, and his lips seemed far more interested in the curve of her neck than an answer.

"She said the old mountain men used to tell stories about folks turning into animals. Like werewolves. Werebears, too."

He stiffened while she circled his ear with her tongue.

"Really?" He said it slowly, carefully, probably wondering what she was going on about.

"Really. People who could change into wolves or bears or other animals. And you know what?" She nudged with her hips again, finding the hard spot she sought in his jeans.

"What?" he croaked.

She looked up at the stars, then dipped down and spoke right into his lips. "The moon isn't out, but I'm kind of feeling the animal urge tonight."

He let out a puff of air and relaxed. "Really? I barely noticed."

She smiled then tested the seam of his lips. They opened, letting her in, and she kissed him deeply, moaning with delight.

"If you could turn into an animal, what would you be?" he asked while working open the top button of her blouse.

"Mmm." She mumbled and got back to work on his ear. "I don't know. What would you be?"

"A bear. Definitely a bear."

"Let me guess." She tickled his ear with a lock of her hair. "A grizzly."

He nodded gravely, tracing her collarbone with his thumb. "What about you?"

"Then I'd have to be a bear, too." She threaded her fingers through his thick hair, clearing a path from his ear to his neck to kiss.

"You wouldn't *have* to be," he pointed out.

God, she loved this man.

"I'd want to be."

His neck tasted even better than his lips, if that was possible. She kissed right down to the hollow under his chin, then went back to his lips to double-check. Maybe she needed more research to decide. Lots more research.

Todd slid his hands from her waist to her rear, bringing her closer. She rolled her hips and watched his eyes close.

"Do that again," he whispered.

Crush herself against the unmistakable ridge of his jeans? Gladly.

"How's that?" she whispered, hiding her own groan of pleasure.

"Good. Too good."

His head tipped back, letting her explore. She pressed big, open-mouthed kisses to the sensitive skin of his neck, sucking as she went.

His hands worked her in long, insistent strokes, going from the lowest part of her ass all the way up to her ribs until she was begging for more.

"Todd..." Now she was the one growling, insisting.

When he unclipped her bra and touched her, she shuddered.

She reared up, whipped off her shirt and bra, and looked at him. Too late to be shy or worried that she was too small. Her breath caught in her throat.

He stroked the side of her breast gently, the roughest part of his thumb to the softest, most sensitive area of her flesh.

"So beautiful," he murmured. "So perfect."

She felt a blush spread over her face. He said it like he meant it.

Of course I mean it, his blue eyes said.

She stretched tall and lowered herself until her nipple was an inch away from his mouth, waiting. Desperate for his touch.

I am ready to take this all the way, the gesture said. *Are you?*

A slow, sultry smile spread across Todd's face. His lips quirked, but he didn't say anything. He just nodded once and opened his mouth, inviting her to come closer.

Come to me, his whole body told her. *Come to me.*

Chapter Nine

It was crazy, stripping with Anna out on the deck like that.

Crazy and oh, so good.

Todd flexed his fingers, hoping she'd get the signal to come a little lower. Yes, he could rise up and taste her, but he needed to be sure she was ready to give.

And give and give and give, his bear prayed.

She dipped a little, letting that perfect pink bead slip past his lips.

Her groan vibrated in his mind, just as loud and clear as all her words had been. That was part of Anna's magic; digging past the physical to the emotional, connecting with more than just words.

His eyes just about rolled back in his head as he closed his lips around her tight nipple. He teased it with his tongue until it was as erect as... as... okay, as he was. And Jesus, he'd have to do something about that soon. But this was too good to rush. Anna's pleasure was his, too, and he wouldn't deny either of them this high.

For a moment, he worried about one of the others finding them there. What if Sarah wandered by and saw them getting it on? What if Soren came out into the back lot to pick up more beer and heard the noise they were bound to make?

He discarded the worry immediately. Shifters had a sixth sense for such things. They'd steer clear to give Anna and him their privacy. God knew how many times he'd detoured around his cousins in their most passionate meetings with their mates. Soren, in all those years with Sarah, and Simon with Jessica. Would they approve?

He turned the thought over for all of two seconds before deciding he didn't give a shit. This was about him and Anna and no one else.

He worked her nipple around and around until she was dancing wildly over him. Then he switched sides and alternated light rubs of his stubbly cheek with soft licks, and she groaned even more.

More, his bear chanted inside. *Please, more.*

He cupped her breast, kneading it, funneling the tight nub toward his mouth until he was gorging on her. Bear-style, like he might with the sweetest honey of summer or the last berries of fall. The way a bear did when he knew winter was coming, and it was going to be long and hard.

The thought hovered over him ominously until he swiped it away. *Later* didn't matter. Not right now.

His hands wandered along her tight, smooth curves — unbearably beautiful curves, from the swell of her ass to the plunging lines beyond that called to his bear.

Must have my woman. Must have her soon.

He worked his hand around until he cupped her mound, and she bucked against him in delight. He popped the button of her jeans, tucked his fingers inside the waistband, and then froze.

Sanity check. Was he really going to strip her right here?

Of course, we're going to strip her right here, his bear snapped back.

Anna wiggled, giving him the green light, and he rolled her jeans and panties away. The second she straddled him, his hips jerked up.

He groaned past the nipple still teasing his mouth and touched her between the legs. The scent of her arousal, together with the slippery moisture greeting his fingers worked him like a one-two punch.

"Yes. . ." she whispered when he probed deeper, exploring her folds.

Her body was tight with muscle, but inside, she was pillow soft. So soft, he might even have thought along the lines of *delicate* if she hadn't been grinding so hard against his hand.

The thought of how good it would feel to bury himself in that sweet heaven almost made him come there and then. But, shit. He froze.

Anna's head popped up, and her hair cascaded back in a silky wave. Her breasts bobbed above his face, pink from the scratch of his stubble.

"What?"

"I don't have a condom."

She dropped back to his chest and made a cooing sound, totally unconcerned. "I'm clean. Believe me, I'm clean."

He shook his head. As a shifter, he couldn't catch or transmit anything. That wasn't the issue. "Still need a condom."

He might let himself get carried away with Anna — Jesus, he couldn't stop himself — but he'd never neglect a condom again. No way.

She shook her head, hiding her face against his chest and whispering the first words he failed to catch that night.

"What?" He stroked her silky skin.

"I can't get pregnant," Anna mumbled.

He stopped moving, but a second later, Anna threw herself back into the rocking motion as if to erase emotion with action. Her voice was casual, unconcerned, but he could hear the pain beneath it.

"You can't..." he echoed stupidly, then shut up.

"Don't stop," she whispered. Desperate, he sensed, to get past the subject. "Please don't stop."

He dragged her head down to his and plunged into a kiss. She wanted distraction? Fine. He'd distract her all night. But sooner or later, he'd work her back to the topic. No way should she keep that kind of pain inside.

First things first, his bear murmured.

He nodded. Yeah, he was okay with that. But he wouldn't forget. Not something as important as that.

All right, then, his bear growled.

He slid his fingers inside her again, getting back to the *distraction* part. And a minute later, when she was huffing and puffing and humming his name, he rolled.

"Time I took the top," he murmured, pinning her with his weight.

She squeaked as he rolled, and he grinned. Did she really think he would lie back and let her do all the work?

Show her. Show her what a bear can do.

He glanced down, taking in the full length of her body for the first time. God, she was perfect. Absolutely perfect.

"Todd..." she breathed, looking at him with wide, wild eyes.

For a brief, ugly second, he remembered his scars and his injuries, but Anna smiled at him at exactly that moment and pushed every worry away.

"Ready to show a girl a good time?"

Oh, he'd show her, all right. Show her until she cried his name and came shuddering in his arms. But he made his bear promise to keep its fangs tucked away for the night first.

No mating bites, you hear me?

Who, me? his bear said all too innocently.

He still wasn't sure he should allow himself this one night, let alone dream of a lifetime together. He couldn't be sure fate wouldn't strike her down to punish him. But damn it, he couldn't stop. No way. Not tonight.

"Ready," he murmured.

She stripped him as fast as he'd stripped her — faster, maybe — and wrapped one hand around his aching cock.

"Yeah, I'd say you're ready," she breathed.

He thrust in her hand in answer to the unspoken challenge. Yeah, he was ready. Was she?

She wrapped one long leg around him then the other, and he swore she dragged it out just to torture him. Her knees parted wide, welcoming him, and her eyes reflected the starlight. God, it was impossible not to imagine *forever*. Forever with this woman who understood him so well. Whose touch could settle his nerves or set him on fire, whichever she desired.

Then he imagined *forever* without her, and a cloud cast a shadow over his soul.

If I'm not allowed to bite, his bear growled, *you're not allowed to think about bad things.*

"Forget about everything else," Anna murmured. "Everything but you and me."

He slid an inch higher, lined up their bodies, and pushed inside her with one smooth thrust.

"Todd..." she cried, clinging to his gaze.

The need that had been an itch became a bonfire that roared through his veins. He pulled back and thrust in. Deeper. Harder.

"Yes..." Her eyes fluttered, and she extended her arms over her head, giving herself over to him completely.

Mine, his bear chanted, urging him along. *Mine.*

He pumped harder, wincing at the searing sensation. She was tight — God, so incredibly tight — and her inner muscles milked him every inch of the way.

"Yes," she murmured, drawing her knees higher along his sides.

He pinned her hands down with his, just as they were begging him to.

"Look at me." He meant to ask, not demand, but the words came out gruff and uncompromising.

Anna locked eyes with him, nodding him along.

Harder, her eyes begged.

He pulled back, took a breath, and hammered back in.

She bared her teeth and tipped her head back but didn't break eye contact.

Deeper. She nodded.

His whole body burned as he thrust into her again.

Please... Please, her whole body seemed to cry.

He set into a rhythm, pumping harder. Every long, hot stroke brought him a step higher to the top of the cliff he wanted to tumble down so badly, he could have screamed.

"Yes... Yes..." Her cries skirted the border of pleasure and pain. Was he going too hard? Pushing too far?

Anna raised her head, reminding him she was no lightweight. Her eyes slid down the narrow gap between their naked chests and focused at a point below his waist.

She's watching, his bear yowled. *She likes it.*

101

He withdrew until his cock strained at her entrance, letting her drink her fill. Then he thrust — really thrust, burying himself to the hilt.

Her eyes glazed over, and she clutched at him, trying a dozen different positions. But the only position that really mattered was the angle of his cock inside her, and when he lifted her hips a little higher and slid home again, her mouth opened in a silent cry.

Her hips pumped in time with his. Her nails scraped his back, and she arched off the ground.

"God, yes..."

He watched a drop of sweat fall from his body to hers. After that, his vision blurred, and everything ceased to exist but the exquisite friction inside. Building higher... higher...

Anna cried and shuddered in his arms, coming apart.

He clamped his hands around her hips a second before his release hit him. Then he was shuddering, too, and panting and pressing his mouth to her skin to suppress his bear's groan of ecstasy.

"Yes..." Anna panted, contracting around him one more time. "Yes..."

Every muscle in his body strained to hold on to his high, yet he'd never felt more at peace.

Mine, his bear rumbled. *Mate.*

Her fingers brushed silky strokes across his back. He listened to her pant into his neck, then realized it was him panting into her neck, and finally decided he couldn't care less who it was. He slumped, letting his body melt into position around her.

"Todd," she murmured. Her voice was muffled, but it sounded pleased. Very pleased.

"Anna," he mumbled, stroking her hair.

Chapter Ten

Anna lay perfectly still, looking at the stars. She would have preferred gazing into Todd's eyes — they were just as deep, just as bright, and just as full of mysteries — but he had his face pressed to her chest, and she wasn't in any hurry for him to move.

"Wow," she murmured when he stirred.

Her heart rate was still galloping away like an out-of-control stagecoach, but it was a distant sensation, just like the feel of him under her hands. The only thing she registered clearly was the heat pulsing between their bodies.

It wasn't heat like the heat of noon, not even in Arizona. Not like heat from a fireplace you could snuggle up to. It was heat from within, and it zipped both of them into a snug little cocoon.

"Wow," Todd agreed. He rolled to his side but kept her close, and he didn't open his eyes.

She stroked his shoulder, wondering about his scars. He had a lot of them. Burn scars slashed one side of his chest. A long, jagged scar ran from his ribs to his hip. They weren't blemishes so much as medals of honor to her eyes. All part of the amazing man she wanted to learn so much more about.

The amazing man she'd just slept with under the stars.

She chuckled.

"What?" he murmured into her neck.

"I'm naked in a public place—"

"Semi-public," he mumbled.

"Wrapped around a naked man. And sweaty. I'm very sweaty."

He looked up.

"In the best possible way," she filled in quickly.

He smiled, immediately ratcheting up her inner furnace another ten degrees, and she couldn't help but wonder how many times he could make her come in one night.

She wondered if she dared find out.

Then she looked into the burning embers that were his eyes and gulped. Was he thinking the same thing?

But as so often happened with Todd, the sparks in his eyes flickered and suddenly dimmed. He snuggled her closer and cupped her face.

"I'm sorry you can't have kids," he said quietly.

She looked away, but the soft stroke of his thumb on her cheek made her look up again. Making her face the truth instead of hiding from it.

"Yeah, well..." She gestured weakly.

Todd didn't inch away as she half expected him to. He didn't give her that disappointed, *Are you sure you tried hard enough?* look her mother always nailed her with. He just looked sad.

"How do you know?" he asked. "Or shouldn't I ask?"

She bit her lip. There were a thousand happy things she'd rather talk to him about. She'd never really talked about the issue with anyone, not even Sarah. Did she really want to ruin a magical night by discussing it now?

She looked up at the stars, and they seemed to say, *If you want him to open up to you, you need to open up to him.*

She scratched her cheek. Slid her hand along his chest. Counted blades of fake grass, then finally got it out.

"My ex and I tried—"

"Your ex?" Todd's voice dropped.

She closed her eyes. Yes, her ex. "Both of us were only twenty-two and barely out of college, but he wanted to start a family right away. So we tried. And tried..." She trailed off. How much to say? How much to gloss over? "I had a miscarriage. Then another. And another."

Todd ran a hand down her shoulder, helping the shake in her voice even out again.

"He didn't get how hard that was. To him, it wasn't a baby until it was born. To me, it was Tasha and Danny and Lucille." A huge lump built in her throat, thinking about the way she used to touch her belly and hope and wish and pray.

She shook her head. If Jeff hadn't understood, why on earth would Todd? God, why had she even told him? He was probably squirming inside, thinking about ways to make a graceful exit while he could.

Well, this has been really nice, he'd say as he rolled away from her and headed for the stairs. *But I think I'd better go...*

Or maybe he'd stay a while but say something crass like, *Why didn't you just try again?*

But he didn't roll away, and he didn't say anything. Not for a long time. And when he did speak, it wasn't aimed at her so much as at the stars.

"I don't get fate." A bitter note snuck into his voice.

The way he said it suggested he'd had his share of dark nights crying into a pillow — or whatever version of grief guys like him unleashed. Maybe hacking big oak trees into tiny little bits? Throwing bricks at a cement wall? She'd never tried those methods, but hell, she'd sure be tempted to.

She sniffled. "Yeah. Well, at least I found out what kind of guy Jeff was when he left."

Todd's head jerked around. "He left?"

She nodded.

"He left you?" His voice took on an incredulous tone. *What idiot would ever leave a woman like you?*

That, at least, made her smile.

"I told him I needed time to regroup before trying again." She shrugged.

"And?" A growl built in Todd's throat. A good thing they weren't at a cocktail party and face-to-face with her ex. She had the feeling Todd would tear out Jeff's throat.

"He said he wanted a divorce. He was married with a baby thirteen months after I lost Lucille."

"What a shithead."

She actually laughed, because it felt good to hear someone else say it out loud. Almost everyone else just looked at her like it had all been her fault. All her mother had done was urge her to beg Jeff to take her back and promise to try any treatment he thought she ought to subject herself to.

Fight for him, honey, her mother had said. *Go back and try again.*

The corners of Todd's mouth turned down, and his eyes grew dark, as if he knew. Really, truly *knew* the feeling of losing a child he'd never even had the chance to meet properly.

She looked into his eyes, wondering just what was going through his mind.

"Hey," she whispered, trying to cheer both of them up. "I was having a good time until now."

He gave her a weak smile and pulled her closer. "Sorry. I was having a good time, too."

"Really?" Her voice squeaked a little.

His smile turned into the genuine thing. "Yeah. And you know what?" He tugged and turned at the same time, pulling her on top of him.

"What?" she said, stretching out along his body. His chest hair tickled her nipples, and her legs tangled with his.

"We're back where we started." His eyes dropped to her lips.

She smiled and shifted her weight slightly, pressing down with her hips. "I guess we are."

One broad hand tugged gently on the back of her neck, pulling her into a kiss. The other slid from her waist to her rear and pressed down.

She sighed into the kiss and split into a straddle. His cock twitched under her, and she sat up over him.

"Mmm," she murmured, flipping her hair back. She put her hands on his chest and started sliding over him in long, languorous strokes. Up then down, nestling closer each time until she was dragging herself over his cock.

She murmured her pleasure and closed her eyes, relishing the feel of him under her. Then she reared back and watched his eyes as she slowly slid down over his cock, taking him deep.

Fill me, she nearly cried. *Fill the emptiness inside. Fill it with your heat.*

Todd wrapped his hands around her waist and pulled her closer. She rolled her hips, taking him deeper.

Fill me like no man ever has before, she wanted to say. He already had, but she was greedy for more.

When he bucked up, she gasped. She leaned farther and farther back, working him deeper, cartwheeling her arms back to grip his thighs. She rode him, totally and utterly exposed. Her breasts bounced, her hair swayed, and the looks Todd gave her made her feel beautiful instead of self-conscious. She rocked harder and harder, losing her breath. Hissing as he stretched her, gasping when he slid against exactly the right spot. Every sharp thrust of his hips seared her inner walls.

He teased her nipples and kneaded her breasts, finding out what drove her wild. Every touch pushed her closer and closer to the edge — but then he'd back off, refusing to let her come.

"Please... please... " She found herself begging.

Her breasts felt tiny in his huge hands but delightfully sensitive to the callused pads of his fingers. And when he snaked his left hand down to stroke her clit, she had to bite her lip to keep from crying out.

"Yes... yes... " She moaned as she rode him, faster and faster, desperate for more. Thank goodness for the noise drifting up from the bar.

She was close. So amazingly close, yet release kept evading her.

"Todd," she moaned, hovering between ecstasy and frustration. Something was missing. Something she couldn't put her finger on. The angle was perfect. His touch, just right. But something—

His hands tightened suddenly, and he rolled them both, coming out on top. And the second she was on her back, he slammed down with his full weight, pushing deep, deep inside her.

Yes was what she wanted to cry, but it came out all garbled and low.

She echoed his movements with desperate pushes on his ass while squeezing with her inner muscles, determined to make it as good for him as it was for her.

With a low grunt, Todd increased the pace. His chest was right over hers, and his chin jutted as he chased the high they both sought.

Then her orgasm hit her, and she just about howled. Every muscle in her body flexed, and Todd groaned, too. He powered through two more thrusts, and then he came, too, shuddering and burning inside her.

He lowered his body and whispered in her ear as aftershocks of pleasure hit her body, one by one. Was he telling her to be quieter? That she was beautiful? That he'd never had a woman like her before? Whatever the words were, they were soft and sweet, and her soul seemed to understand perfectly, even though her brain couldn't quite make out the individual sounds.

Todd nuzzled while he whispered. At first, she thought it was just a nice cover-up for the awkward task of wiping them both off with his T-shirt, but it went on much longer than that. He started by nuzzling around her right cheek, and when she expected him to break away, he switched to the other side and went on. And on and on. When she managed to coax her blissed-out mind back into gear, it occurred to her that he was going about it in a systematic way, working from low to high and right to left until every square inch of her skin was pink and glowing.

"You trying to shed a second skin off on me?" She giggled as he worked his way down her neck.

"Something like that," he murmured, scraping his stubble along her collarbone.

It felt so good, she closed her eyes and hummed. But then her legs got dangerously close to wrapping around him again, and he slowly eased away from her to stand. Behind him, the stars of the Great Bear glittered even brighter than before.

"Come on," he said, pulling her to her feet.

"Whoa." She grabbed his arms for balance. "Wait, I kind of like it up here on the deck."

He wrapped her tightly in his arms, and she could feel his cock harden against her side. "I like it too much. Come on. Let's go to bed."

108

Chapter Eleven

"So, you and Anna, huh?" Soren raised his eyebrows.

Todd growled at his cousin. Never mind that Soren was handing him a coffee and muffin like every other morning. Never mind that any shifter in a five-mile radius could smell Anna's scent on him. He really, really wasn't ready to discuss it.

Todd took a bite of his muffin and spoke through the crumbs. "None of your business."

"True." Soren nodded thoughtfully, then scratched his chest. "But you still have to tell her, you know. Or were you thinking this is just a short-term thing?"

His bear nearly roared out loud, and his canines extended from his gums in the most blatant challenge he'd ever pulled to Soren's higher rank.

"Not a short-term thing," he growled.

"Yeah, I figured as much," Soren murmured.

"You figured what?"

"I figured fate brought you here for something other than fixing up the bar," he mused, watching the steam rising from his mug.

Todd stared. "You figured? And you were going to tell me — when?"

Soren just shrugged. "Gotta figure it out yourself. That's the way it is with fate."

Fate. A four-letter word as far as he was concerned.

Soren motioned toward the café with his mug. Anna was in there, helping Jessica with the morning shift.

"You have to tell her. You have to explain about who we are. What we are. What it means for her."

He'd have told Soren to take a hike if it weren't for the fact that he'd given his cousin the same lecture years ago when the tables were turned. And Christ, it had taken ages for Soren to finally tell Sarah.

Todd slumped over the table they sat at in the closed saloon. Yes, Anna was his mate. Yes, she was amazing. And yes, he could barely stand letting her step out of his sight this morning. That part was easy to understand.

The hard part was being honest — not just about being a shifter, but about other things, too. Like the truth about Teddy. So far, he hadn't told Anna because it wasn't the kind of thing you blurted out to a perfect stranger. *By the way, let me tell you the long, sad story about how I came to be the father of a child I will never be able to call my own.* You just didn't do that kind of thing.

But a woman you were serious enough about to want *forever* with *had* to know that kind of thing. And crap — things had moved so quickly between them that he hadn't really had a chance to explain. He really ought to have told her before last night.

"I know I have to tell her," he said. "The question is how."

And that was just one part of it. The other was the even bigger picture. He still couldn't figure out whether fate was actually giving him a choice or just fucking with him again.

A choice. His bear nodded firmly.

Fucking with me, his human side said.

"And what about..." he started, then trailed off.

"What about what?" Soren asked.

He shook his head. No, he wasn't going to say the next part aloud. But he sure as hell couldn't help thinking it. Maybe Anna was better off without him. Humans didn't spend a lifetime longing for their mates the way shifters did. Sure, humans fell in love, but they fell out just as easily. Even if she was okay with the bear part — and Christ, how would he ever explain that? — and even if she agreed to be his mate, she'd be stuck forever with a bear who was all scarred up. He could hardly hear—

Can hear her perfectly, his bear cut in.

Sure, he heard her. But that was about all he heard. He'd nearly gotten run over by a car the other day, and the driver had shaken a fist at him like he was some kind of idiot not to get out of the way. That's what she'd be stuck with. A half-deaf guy with a half-functioning hand.

She sure didn't seem to mind last night.

He scowled. *It wasn't about making her feel good—*

It isn't?

He rolled his eyes, but his bear persisted. *Like Uncle Connor used to say. Love is making your mate happy, because that makes you happy, too.*

Todd sighed. He was pretty sure Uncle Connor hadn't been talking about sex.

We can make her happy in lots of other ways, too.

The problem was, he'd bet lots of guys could make her happy.

Who? his bear demanded. *Someone like that ass, Jeff?*

No, like any one of the half-dozen guys who eyed her closely whenever she walked by. Who wouldn't look? The way she moved, the way she spoke. The way her eyes smiled *into* you like you were someone special and not just anyone—

Maybe she just does that for us.

Todd shook his head. There had to be at least four guys hanging out in the café right now, shooting Anna smiles and chatting her up every chance they got. A constant stream of wolf shifters rotated through the café since Ty Hawthorne had stepped up the watch system — ostensibly to keep an eye on things. But Todd knew that most of those guys took that to mean keeping a close eye on the women — especially the unmated ones. And there were all those overfriendly human customers, too.

"Man, don't make the mistake I did," Soren said.

He looked up warily.

"Don't let your mate go." Soren's face grew somber. "I nearly lost Sarah." His voice was low and gritty. "I nearly lost everything."

I already have lost everything, Todd wanted to say.

111

He crumpled up his napkin and stood. That morning, he'd woken up feeling like he could leap over the saloon in a single bound. Now, he felt creaky and spent. Recognizing his mate was easy. Knowing what to do about it was the hard part.

"Where you going?" Soren arched an eyebrow.

Where else? He pointed toward the back room. Maybe an hour of sanding would help him figure something out.

Soren shook his head and took the last sip of his coffee, then stood. "Not today. Jessica and Sarah really want the garage finished. We need to clear the last of the junk out."

"Now?"

Soren shrugged and headed out. "The baby's napping. No better time."

Such a simple statement, yet one that prompted such a heavy feeling of loss. Todd scowled as he followed Soren out the back. He was just a puppet in fate's hands. A tool. Why would he ever drag Anna into a life as messed up as that?

"All this crap has to go," Soren said, motioning toward the heap in the garage.

Todd wondered if it was time for him to go, too.

Gotta stay. Gotta keep our mate safe.

"We're only keeping the useful stuff," Soren went on.

He nodded quietly. Yeah, he got the message. Right now, he was useful. But as soon as they tracked down that rogue wolf and ensured the clan's safety, he'd be superfluous, too. Just like the dusty black-and-white TV set he carried on the first trip over to Soren's truck or the boxes of old magazines. They'd had their day to shine. Now they were faded and worn.

A lot like him.

"On three," Soren said, and they both lifted a steel workbench covered in cobwebs. There was a lot of sawdust, too, and the smell transported him to the mill at home.

Home. Maybe he would head back to Montana, after all. He could go back to bear form and live in a den, or he could fix up a cabin somewhere way out in the woods.

Not going anywhere without Anna, his bear growled.

"I can't understand what the previous owners ever did with all this stuff," Soren sighed. There were empty jars, snowshoes, and even a set of golf clubs.

Todd eyed the clutter. Yeah, there was a lesson in that. Whatever he decided to do, he'd keep it simple.

A vision flashed before his eyes: him, sitting on the porch of a painfully empty cabin, stroking a long, gray beard. Jesus, he'd turn into one of those loony hermits the mountains were full of.

Just talk to her, his bear said.

Soren pulled one of the golf clubs out and swung it like a bat. "Maybe we should keep one of these around. Keep the troublemakers away." Then he laughed and stuck it in the back of the pickup. "Of course, bear claws work pretty well for that, too."

Todd flexed his right hand involuntarily. Yeah, bear claws were good if they worked, but he wasn't sure he could extend his.

Soren's head snapped right, and he jogged over to the saloon. Either the baby had just woken up, or the phone was ringing. Whatever it was, Todd hadn't heard it. He itched to pull out the glass jars and throw them against the wall one by one. Instead, he settled for slamming a rusty old rake into the back of the pickup. Then he looked around for something else to smash, bend, or break, but all he found was an old Formica countertop. He was just thumping it into the truck when Soren came out with Teddy in his arms.

When Soren stepped close, Teddy reached a hand out to grab Todd's ear, and he froze. His son, reaching out to him? For him?

The baby stopped short and grabbed Soren's beard instead.

"Little rug rat," Soren murmured, nuzzling the baby with his chin.

Todd dropped his gaze. Yeah, he got the picture, all right. An idyllic father-son relationship he played no part in. All he could do was ruin it.

"You mind if we finish up later?" Soren asked, turning away. "Little guy's hungry. Gotta go find Mommy. Right,

113

Teddy?"

Todd watched them go, aching inside. No, he'd never be a part of that baby's life. But he couldn't just walk away, either. He needed the baby to know he cared.

His eyes rose to the deck on the second floor. Whatever happened, he needed Anna to know he cared about her, too. He tapped his fingers against his thigh. Laying the Astroturf had been step one of a bigger plan. It was time for step two.

And step three, his bear murmured, adding a dozen new ideas to the plan. *And four and five and six.*

He hesitated, but his bear was adamant. *Come on. Go get her. What do we have to lose?*

How about the last remaining bit of his pride? The last vestiges of honor? The tiny kernel of hope she'd planted in his heart?

You saying she's not worth it? his bear goaded.

He growled under his breath. He'd risk anything for her.

Then do it. Hurry up already.

Two seconds later, he was heading for the back door of the café.

Chapter Twelve

Anna had skipped coffee that morning, because she was already running on an energy kick of the very best kind. Even the hours she spent on her feet waitressing didn't wipe the stupid grin off her face.

She hadn't actually walked into the café that morning announcing, *Wow, what a night,* but she knew it had to be written all over her face. The others were kind enough not to say anything, although she did catch the occasional knowing smile.

Yep. I did it, she wanted to say. *I finally slept with the man I've been obsessing about.*

Of course, having spent the night with Todd only made her obsess even more, because she was dying to see him again. To make an excuse to cross paths with him and maybe sneak in a secret kiss.

Or two. Or three. Or ten.

She almost wished someone would come out and ask her about her night so she could say it out loud. Something like, *Yes, I really did strip naked on the deck last night. Yes, it was incredible. And yes, he's as sweet and generous a lover as I thought he would be.*

Nobody asked, so she didn't get to sing Todd's praises, but she did hum as she moved.

You know what the best part was? She cued her imaginary audience to ask and immediately filled in the answer. *This morning.*

She'd been snoozing in that deeply satisfied state only a woman who'd orgasmed multiple times in a few short hours could. She barcly stirred when Todd woke, but she still remembered it all. He'd kissed her on the forehead and murmured something she didn't quite catch, though it made her grin. He stood at the doorway watching her for a long time before he left, and though she hadn't been able to keep her eyes open the whole time, she could feel him there. Watching. Protecting. Dreaming of what might be.

God, she wanted more mornings like that. Mornings that spelled out the definition of *serene*. The peace and quiet stayed with her even when the café bustled with action. Some customers were worried, others just hurried. She wanted to laugh and tell them to slow down.

"Can I get a refill, please?" a customer asked, prodding her back into action.

"I got it," Janna said, already coming her way with a steaming pot of coffee. "Can you get that?"

The phone in the back of the café was ringing, and she grabbed it after the fourth or fifth ring.

"Quarter Moon Café. Hello?"

Too late, it seemed. The line went dead.

She was just turning back to the café when the back door opened. A bolt of sunlight streamed into the kitchen, backlighting a man.

Her heart leaped. Actually, her legs did, too, and before she could think, she'd dashed across the kitchen, into Todd's arms, and straight into a kiss.

A kiss that was a taste of heaven, what with the golden light filling the space around him and around her soul.

"Hey," she whispered when she finally mustered enough control to pull back an inch. She meant to pull back a whole foot to a more chaste position, but that much control was a little too much to ask for just then.

"Hey," he whispered. A tiny smile played around his lips, but his eyes were worried. Why?

"You good?" She tilted her head to one side, studying his face.

He combed her hair back with his fingers. "Good." He nodded. "But I need your help."

She bit her lip so it wouldn't tremble and nodded. She knew enough about the Voss clan to know it was a rare moment, indeed, to have one of those proud men trust someone enough to ask for help.

He held both her arms, and she wondered what he'd ask her to do. Jump off a cliff? Confront the ghosts of his past? Move to Montana and marry him? Whatever it was, she was all in.

"There's a hard part and an easy part," he said, squeezing her hands tighter.

"Anything," she said.

Anything? a little voice in her head asked.

She thought it over briefly, then nodded to herself. Yes, she'd vowed not to be careless and lose her heart to a man again. But Todd wasn't any man, so she could make an exception for him.

"Anything," she whispered.

Slowly, he brought her hand to his mouth and kissed her knuckles. His eyes flashed and sparked with a hundred secret wishes, and she wanted to make them all come true.

"Okay, then," he said, looking over her shoulder. "Can you come now?"

"I have to ask Jess—" she started, then stopped, chagrined to see that Jessica had entered the kitchen.

Jessica looked ridiculously pleased to see the two of them together. "Sure she can. Go." She shooed them toward the door.

Anna pulled her apron off and slid her fingers around his. "Okay, then. Where are we going?"

"I need your advice on getting a few things," he murmured, leading her to the car.

He didn't say much more than that, and though she was dying of curiosity, she held her tongue. Men like Todd were like the mountains in spring — they didn't thaw overnight, and you sure couldn't rush them. So she forced herself to be patient and relish the tiny little signals he gave off. His fingers played over hers as they drove, and when he peeked over from time to time, she caught his soft gaze lingering on her hair. Her eyes.

117

And her lips. His eyes kept darting back to her lips, and even though it wasn't a hungry, *I-can't-wait-another-minute* look like the ones he'd given her the previous night, it still made her inner animal roar.

She hid a grin. So much for men being the ones to obsess about sex. She was the dirty-minded one.

Todd's nostrils flared, and for a second, she wondered if she'd emitted some secret signal that gave her away. His hand flexed over hers and his lips moved, but he kept his cool.

"The hardware store?" she asked as he motioned for her to pull the car they'd borrowed into a huge parking lot. Not Mike's Hardware, but one of those huge megastores. He needed her help here?

He nodded quietly but didn't say a thing until they entered and wove their way to a section all the way at the back.

"So, what do you think?" he murmured.

His hands were stuck deep in his pockets, and the look on his face was that of a man preparing to slap down his life savings for the biggest purchase of his life. Yet he was pointing to... a kiddie pool?

"It's kind of small, but I think it would fit on the deck," he said.

She looked at the tiny blue basin with its starfish design. "I think it's perfect. Like a tiny lake or something. A little piece of Montana brought right to the baby's home."

His mouth fell open as if surprised to find her sharing his vision. But it was written all over his face. The Astroturf was more than an artificial version of grass; it represented a piece of his home. The pool represented the cool, clear creeks that babbled over boulders and rocks, and the awning he found next was the shade of the forest.

"I know it's not Montana," he said a little sheepishly once they were back on the deck behind the saloon. It took them a few hours, but they got everything set up. "But it reminds me of home. And Arizona's okay, but a bear—" he stuttered a little, correcting himself "—a baby needs other things, too."

He brought in a lounge chair and an end table and a bunch of leafy plants — tall, spiky yuccas and rich green plumeria that provided both shade and privacy, even if they had been a bitch to get up the stairs.

"It's beautiful. Teddy will have his own mountain meadow. His own summer creek. . . "

"Now I just need to find a way to plant some berries so he can pick them in the fall," Todd whispered, scanning their work with an inscrutable look.

Something in her jumped at the echo of words she knew she'd heard before. Were they words *she'd* said before? She couldn't remember — not with her mind busy picking through so many other memories. Like all the times she'd itched to set up her own backyard play area for a baby she never got to bring home.

She ran a hand across her brow, wondering why it didn't make her cry. She'd come close a few times already — when Todd adjusted the angle of the slide so it was just right, or when he murmured something about a baby that wasn't her own.

Much as her heart ached, though, it also rejoiced. All the loving things she'd never gotten to do for the babies she'd lost, she was getting to do now. And while part of her wanted to wail, it felt good at the same time. To finally face the loss. To work through it. To shape something for her own babies with her own hands, even though it was only symbolic. Her ex hadn't been into decorating nurseries or picking out strollers, and after losing the first baby, she'd been so afraid to jinx things that she'd held back from the normal nesting rituals. The nursery remained an empty, white-walled room, the yard didn't change from being a plain square of green, and the ache in her heart stayed locked away.

But now, she slowly pushed that creaky door open and took a good look around.

She blinked back the tears for a few minutes, then nodded to herself and shut that door again. She didn't bother with the lock this time because she knew she'd be visiting that place again. No use in pretending the pain wasn't there, because it was intertwined with love. And that, she didn't want to lock away.

Todd slung an arm over her shoulders and looked over the deck with her. He had a sad, faraway look in his eyes, but a weary kind of satisfaction, too. They'd set up the pool, a tiny little slide, and a wooden bench for Sarah or Soren to sit on while bouncing the baby in their arms. The awning had been the hardest part to install, but they'd managed to bolt in anchor points and stretch it overhead. They left the last bit of deck unshaded, though.

"A place for the baby to look at the stars," Todd had said when she asked why.

She pictured him describing the constellations to little Teddy someday and sighed.

"You're the best uncle ever," she said, making a last-minute word change. *You'd make a great dad, too,* had been on the tip of her tongue. But that was a dangerous place for a woman in her state of mind to venture, so she'd reeled the thoughts back.

"Yeah, well." Todd looked over the deck then nodded to himself. "That was the easy part." He led her over to the bench and sank down on it, looking as if he'd aged a decade in the few seconds that had passed.

She sat, trying not to fidget or stare as he worked his jaw. His Adam's apple bobbed, and his fingers flexed. If all that work was the easy part, what was the hard part?

He leaned forward a little, still holding her hand, and whispered, "I need you to know something."

Her breath caught in her throat. God, he was so serious all of a sudden. What was wrong?

"Teddy is Soren and Sarah's, and he always will be. But he's my son. My biological son," he said quickly, stumbling over the words.

She stared at him, grappling with an equation her mind wasn't ready to solve. How could Teddy be Todd's son?

"I slept with Sarah. Once." He shook his hand. "Neither of us really understood why at the time. It just sort of of... happened." His nails scratched his jeans ferociously. Clearly, that explanation didn't satisfy him.

It didn't satisfy her, either. He'd slept with her cousin? That was ridiculous. Sarah had always been devoted to Soren. It couldn't be—

She froze the thought there, remembering that the two had broken up for a time. Her heart thumped in her chest as she pictured it. Sarah had slept with Todd during that time?

She gulped, wondering if it had been Todd who'd come on to Sarah or Sarah who'd come on to Todd. Wondering whether they'd lain side by side and looked at the stars. Jesus, had he showed her the constellations, too?

Anna was sitting close enough to Todd for their legs to touch, but she pushed herself away, leaving a gap. A lump filled her throat, making her words an uneven squeak. "Did last night just happen, too?"

"No!" He reached for her hand, but she snatched it back. "No, Anna. Last night was totally different. That's why I'm telling you."

To torture her? Was that why he was telling her?

"Please. Please listen," he said, squatting down in front of her.

There was no way past that bulk, so she sat perfectly still, arms crossed over her chest. The sound of a freight train roared in her ears, and her cheeks burned. Yes, she was mad. Smoking mad. But part of her was melting for him at the same time. If she took all the times in the past weeks that he'd looked mournful and multiplied it by ten, he still wouldn't have looked as wounded as he did right now.

His voice shook. His hands, too, telling her it wasn't an act.

"What happened with Sarah was a one-time thing. With you, it's totally different. It's my heart, not my..."

Your body? she wanted to grunt, trying to banish the image of his hips pumping over Sarah's. She buried her face in her hands. "Why are you telling me this? Why?"

"Because I don't want it coming between us. I don't want anything coming between us. Ever. I never want to keep a secret from you."

"And how about Sarah's secret?" she couldn't help retorting.

"It's not a secret. Soren knows. He's accepted it. He knew that..."

When Todd trailed off, she wanted to scream. What could Soren possibly know about his cousin screwing hers that made it okay? What kind of twisted love triangle had it all been?

"Look, Soren and Sarah belong together. I'd never come between them."

So why did you sleep with her? she wanted to yell.

"I didn't even know there was a baby, and they thought I was dead..."

Now she was really confused. She'd spent the last months thinking Sarah was dead. Why would Sarah have thought Todd was dead?

"I got here the day you did. Jesus, Anna. What we have is totally different."

She thought it was different, too. She'd felt it in her bones, in her heart. But what if she was wrong?

"Anna." A soft voice came from the door to the apartment, and her head snapped up. It was Sarah, holding the baby.

Anna buried her face in her hands. God, she couldn't face it. Her own cousin had slept with the man she wanted for herself? Rationally, she knew it shouldn't matter. It had happened months before she'd even met Todd, so it was hardly a betrayal. But she couldn't get past that being-late-to-the-party feeling. That gut-sinking feeling of everyone being in on a terrible secret except her.

"Anna, I'm so sorry..." Sarah whispered.

Todd was sorry. Sarah was sorry. Was she supposed to be sorry, too?

"Let me explain..."

She stood quickly. Maybe later, she could sit quietly and soak in an explanation. But right now, she couldn't do it. Right now, all the demons of her past were welling up and taking over.

"I gotta go," she blurted, scurrying past Sarah's outstretched arm.

"Anna—" her cousin cried.

"Anna—" Todd called, but she hurried through the door to the apartment and down the stairs.

Regroup. She needed to regroup. She made a beeline for her car but pulled up short. It was blocked by Soren's pickup, which was filled with yet another load of junk to give away.

The deck overlooked the back lot, and the baby started crying.

She cried, too. That was Todd's baby. Todd's son. With Sarah.

God, she had to get away for a little while. She needed space to pry apart the emotions that were battling in her soul. Old ones, new ones. All her recent hopes lay shattered and sprinkled with pain.

She jumped into the truck and gunned it to life. Soren wouldn't mind. She'd driven a load to the salvage place earlier that week, so she knew the way. What better form of therapy could she find than throwing things? She could already hear the satisfying screech of metal against cement, the blast of shattered glass. A perfect substitute for screaming at the top of her lungs.

Todd emerged from the building looking so hurt, so ragged, she nearly stopped. But she'd already started backing the truck out of its spot, and making the transition to forward and driving away was an instinctual thing. Before she even had time to think it over, she was halfway around the turn.

When she glanced back, Todd was already out of sight.

Concentrate on the road, damn it! She blinked the tears out of her eyes and clutched the wheel harder.

Regroup. Just need a little time to regroup.

But no matter how many times she told herself that, it still felt like a lie.

Chapter Thirteen

Todd sprinted around the corner and down the street then slowed to a jog. He stood panting at the intersection of the alley and the main street, watching Anna leave while his bear ravaged and roared inside.

Don't stop! Get her! Don't let her go!

He didn't want to let her go, but running after her wouldn't help, either.

Neither does standing here, scratching your head. Do something! his bear screamed.

What could he do? Chase her down? Tie her up? Force her to listen to a truth that disgusted him as much as it disgusted her?

He turned back for the saloon, kicking a trash can on the way. The metal lid clattered to the ground and the can tipped on its side, but he left it. And why not? Every time he tried to do the right thing, he screwed up. Why bother trying any more?

Soren came prowling out of the alley, but Todd strode on. He was not backing down for anyone today.

"Whoa," Soren grunted as their shoulders collided. "Hey!"

Todd ignored the thump and hammered on, heading down the alley. No way was he stopping to talk now.

He forced his chin up and gauged the distance to the hills surrounding town. It wouldn't take too long to get out there at this hammering trot of a walk. When he got there, he could disappear deep into the woods, shift into bear form, and maul a few trees. He'd walk as far as his legs could take him and then walk a little more. Maybe he'd walk all the way back to Montana. Starting tonight.

Sick of this, he let himself rage. *I'm so sick of this.*

He was sick of fate giving then taking away. It was turning into a cruel game, and he was tired of playing along. What purpose was there in being the good guy when it only got him screwed over and over again?

Behind him, metal rattled against asphalt as Soren righted the trash can and hurried after him.

Todd flicked his fingers, loosening his claws. Let Soren try to talk some sense into him now.

"Todd," Soren said, using his nice-guy voice instead of his alpha growl.

Yeah, well, Todd wasn't going to fall for that, either.

"Todd," Soren said, more sharply this time.

He barreled on, intent on getting away.

"Hey," Soren said, grabbing his shoulder.

Todd spun with a snarl — a real bear snarl, letting bear claws emerge from his fingers to slice the air an inch in front of his cousin's face.

"Whoa." Soren stopped and stuck his hands in the air.

Todd was about to spin and resume his march to the hills when he caught sight of his claws. He froze, looking at them. Claws. All his claws were out. The ones on his injured hand, too.

He flexed and straightened his fingers, suddenly distracted from the rage that had taken over his mind.

Hey. They work! His bear cheered.

A moment later, he retracted them and started walking again. So his hand had recovered slightly. So what? It wasn't as if that would help him make up with Anna. It wouldn't restore his hearing or turn back the clock on all the other regrets that loomed over him like a dark winter cloud.

"You had to tell her," Soren said, calling after him.

Too bad that trash can was out of range. He'd have liked to give it a few more kicks.

A car rumbled into gear behind them, and he turned to see Simon heading out in another vehicle.

"I told him to follow her," Soren said. "Just in case."

Todd cursed. God, how could he have let the rogue wolf slip his mind?

"We still don't know who it was," Soren said, glaring at the traffic flashing across the intersection at the end of the alley. "Until we do, we have to keep every member of this clan safe."

Todd stared at his cousin. Had he just implied that Anna was a member of this clan?

Soren shrugged, reading his mind. "She could be."

The words hung in the dry air, and for a second, Todd nearly let himself hope again. That Anna would forgive him and come back again. That she'd give him another chance and maybe even accept his bear. They could—

"You know we'd welcome her," Soren said, breaking the spell.

He scuffed the asphalt with his boot. Crap. There he went, believing in the impossible again. Even if that happened, fate would find a way to screw things up for him again.

"Listen," Soren said, then stopped when the phone in his pocket rang. He pulled it out with a scowl and a curt, "Hello?"

Todd thought about continuing his run-walk for the hills, but the look on Soren's face stopped him.

"Where? When? Are you sure it's him?" Soren barked.

He watched his cousin's lips move, wishing he could catch the voice on the other end of the line.

"We'll be right there," Soren finished, hanging up. "That was Zack."

Zack, Twin Moon pack's best tracker?

Soren's face was grim. "He found Roy's trail. He needs you to confirm if that's the wolf who jumped Sarah and Anna last week." He motioned Todd back to the saloon.

Todd nearly let his claws out again. If this Roy guy turned out to be the one who'd threatened Anna last week, he'd kill him, no questions asked.

He caught up with Soren, whose brow was heavily furrowed. "Christ. If it wasn't Roy, we have a problem. We still don't know who the rogue was."

Todd sniffed the air, suddenly glad Simon had gone after Anna. If that rogue was still in the area, he didn't want Anna out there on her own.

"But, shit," Soren went on. "If it was Roy, we have a problem, too. The wolves of Twin Moon Ranch won't like us hunting down one of their own."

Not even a rogue who ambushes our women in the woods? he wanted to protest.

A police car pulled up at the end of the alley, and the man driving it looked equally grim. It was Kyle, a Twin Moon wolf who was also a state cop.

"Get in," he said, nodding them into the back. "I'll take you to the spot where Zack picked up the trail. You think you can tell if it's a match with the wolf who stalked Sarah on that hike?"

Todd's bear growled. *The wolf who stalked Anna on that hike.*

"If it's the same wolf, I'll know."

Soren motioned Kyle back onto the road. "Let's go track this bastard. Now."

Chapter Fourteen

Anna sped down the main road out of town, as angry with herself as she was with the situation. God, she hadn't overreacted, had she?

She sat straighter in the driver's seat and dug her nails into the soft leather of the steering wheel. Okay, she'd definitely overreacted back there. Todd looked so hurt, so lost. Maybe she should have stayed.

But he'd hurt her, damn it. Did he expect her to sit and nod and say okay?

Her phone vibrated in her pocket, and she dug it out quickly, hoping it might be Todd.

The caller's number was hidden so she clicked on the incoming text, switching her focus from the road to the phone and back again.

Car broke down. Can you come pick me up? — Janna.

Janna? Hadn't she left the café earlier for an afternoon out with Cole?

Apparently, she had, and that beaten-up little Ford had died on her again.

Another text beeped through, and the red light she reached lasted just long enough to let her read.

Arizona Road 9257, it said. *Mile marker 11.*

Anna didn't know the area well, but she was pretty sure she'd seen the turnoff to 9257 when she'd driven to the national forest with Sarah.

"There's a reservoir down there," Sarah had said, pointing it out. "Some bald eagle nests, too."

She wondered what Janna was doing all that way down there. But then again, with Janna, you never knew. Maybe she and Cole wanted to check out the eagles?

The light switched green, and she made a last-minute left turn. She'd miss the salvage place by taking this detour first, but it could wait, she supposed. She did a double take in the rearview mirror as she turned. Was that Simon in the car four vehicles back?

But then a truck rumbled past, and she'd made the turn so quickly, the car disappeared from view. Was Simon on the way to help Janna? But if he was, he'd just missed the turn.

She shook her head. It couldn't be. She was just imagining things.

At the next red light, she keyed in her reply. *On my way. See you soon.*

It didn't take long to escape the busy central part of town and join the highway heading north. The turn to the side road was exactly where she thought it would be. She'd never been down that road before, and it turned out to be much narrower and rougher than she assumed. After two bumpy miles, the asphalt petered out to dirt, and she slowed to a crawl. The truck creaked around turn after turn, making the junk in the back rattle so loudly, she wanted to shout. She stopped to text Janna again, but she'd hit a patch with no satellite connection. And no wonder, considering the steep, rocky hills that hemmed in the road.

She counted down the miles, tapping her fingers on the steering wheel. After mile marker 10, the road curved slowly, and when it straightened, she saw Janna's car parked in a little pullout by the trailhead. Actually, there were three cars: Janna's little Ford — that had to be it, even though Anna swore Janna's car was yellow and not red — plus two other vehicles parked at the far end of the small pullout. One was a van with tinted windows left slightly open — and man, that must have had a hell of a time getting out this far. The other was a big rig pickup with Kansas plates.

She'd half expected to find Janna leaning casually against her car, but there was no one to be seen. Anna parked, got out of the truck slowly, and looked around. A hawk cried overhead. The wind stirred the parched grass on the hillsides.

"Janna?" she called, turning in a circle. Had she gone off bird watching while waiting for help?

The car looked okay, with no steam rising from the hood, so that was a good sign. But where was Janna? Where was Cole? The owners of the other vehicles were nowhere to be seen, either. Maybe they'd gone hiking for the day.

"Janna?" she called a little louder.

Her voice echoed faintly off the rocky bluffs.

"Over here!" the delayed reply came.

Anna walked a few steps and looked around.

"Janna?" she called, more quietly this time as uncertainty hit her. Why didn't Janna come out? Why did her voice waver like that?

A thousand scary possibilities hit her at once. Maybe Janna had gone scrambling over the rocks in search of an eagle's nest and fallen. Or maybe Cole had been bitten by a rattlesnake. Sarah had said rattlers weren't that big a danger on the hike they'd done, but that was a forested area and this was drier, open space.

She glanced around. An open, eerie place.

"Over here!" the voice came again, choked and more urgent this time.

The hair prickled on the back of her neck, and she hesitated. Maybe this wasn't such a good idea. But if Janna and Cole were out there and one of them was hurt, she had to do something. She checked her phone. Still no reception.

"Please!" the voice begged.

There was a rake sticking out of the heap of junk in the back of the truck, and she nearly pulled it out. But then she spotted an old set of golf clubs and took one instead. It seemed silly, carrying a piece of sports equipment through the scrubby landscape, but heck, if there were snakes out there, she ought to carry something, right?

"Janna? Cole? Are you okay?" She walked a few steps toward a cluster of rocks where the voice came from. A stand of thorny acacia blocked her way around the right side of the rocks, but a narrow path led around the left side, so she headed that way, picking her way slowly. The last thing she needed was a twisted ankle or a snake bite. Finally, she pushed aside a branch and came out into an open space, where she pulled up short.

A woman stood stiffly with her back to a tree, her face hidden by harsh shadows. But even in the mottled effect of the light, it was obvious that wasn't Janna. This woman was shorter, and her hair was fairer than Janna's. Anna took one more step then froze.

The young woman's face was streaked with tears, and a red bruise marred the left side of her face. Her hands were behind her body, as if—

"I'm so sorry," the woman whispered at the very moment Anna realized she'd been tied to the tree.

Anna jerked back a step and gaped.

"Where's Janna?" she asked, confused.

"They made me do it. I had to play along to save the others."

Anna gasped. Jesus, she'd been tricked. It hadn't been Janna calling for her. It was this stranger, luring her out here. But why?

The young woman's head jerked to one side, and when she looked back at Anna, her eyes were desperate and wide. "Run!" she called hoarsely. "Run! Get away!"

It took Anna a second to react, but when something started crashing through the bushes, she bolted back in the direction of the road. Whatever was happening, she had to get to the truck and get away. She had to get someplace where she could call for help.

Two steps before she reached the path around the boulders, the shadows overhead flickered, and a man leaped right into the path before her.

"Hold it!" he yelled.

She gasped and backpedaled, then froze as the man slowly straightened from the crouch he'd landed in.

"Don't! Emmett, please!" the woman behind her cried.

Anna spun to see the young woman strain at her bonds, but then she turned back to face the man. Now that he was upright, he was an inch taller than her. In any other situation, she'd have thought him unremarkable in every way — except for the pale gray eyes and the scar running vertically from his lip.

"We meet again." He grinned.

Emmett LeBlanc? The man who'd asked about Sarah back in Montana? The man who wanted to kill the bear?

"Now, you were supposed to tell me if you heard anything from your cousin or those Voss brothers," he said, speaking as if in the middle of a conversation and not out of the blue.

She gaped at him. Was he nuts?

He tut-tutted at her, shaking a finger. "I told you to tell me."

Jesus, he really was nuts.

She backed up. "I don't know what you're talking about."

He didn't acknowledge her words. He just went on in that menacing voice. "Now if you'd listened to me, you could have avoided all this."

Her hand tightened around the golf club. All what?

"The others have to die, but you could have lived."

A chill ran through her shoulders. He wanted her to die?

"They're the ones who are unpure. You were innocent."

What the hell was he talking about?

He sniffed the air and scowled. "But now you, too, have crossed the line."

"Emmett, she didn't do anything!" the woman begged from behind her.

Anna swiveled her head between them. Was the woman the man's accomplice or his enemy?

He gestured wildly and screamed. "She's whored herself to that bear! You can smell him all over her!"

"You're crazy," Anna retorted, shaking her head. He was bat-shit crazy, and he wanted her dead.

Think! Act! Flee! Alarms flashed through her mind, paralyzing her completely.

133

"Now, don't think I'm not grateful to you for leading me to the others..." Emmett went on.

God, did he want to kill Sarah and Jessica, too? She could see the blood lust in his eyes. But why? What did they do?

He took a step closer, and Anna jumped back, raising the golf club like a sword.

Emmett laughed. Cackled was more like it, and the sound carried over the harsh landscape.

"Whatcha gonna do with that, honey?"

Club your brains out, she wanted to shout. But her hand shook and her knees wobbled, and he laughed again.

"You don't want to mess with me, honey."

"You don't want to mess with me," she barked through clenched teeth.

Anger flashed in his eyes as he studied her. "You know, I was going to go easy on you." His eyes traveled the length of her body, making her skin crawl. "I was going to make it quick. But maybe I'll teach that bear a lesson." He nodded to himself, considering some new plan. "Wouldn't it just drive him crazy to find out he wasn't the last man who fucked that little human of his?"

"Leave her alone!" the young woman screamed.

Anna didn't know whether to run or hold her ground or strike out before the madman did.

Do something! her whole body screamed.

The young woman sounded desperate enough to be an ally, but Anna didn't have time to free her. The path out was narrow, so she couldn't fake a move in one direction then dart in another to get around Emmett.

"Don't bother. You're gonna die," he said in a flat tone. Like it was inevitable. Mechanical. Impossible to avoid. "And the others, too. Every single one of them."

Her mind flashed with images of Sarah and the others. Jessica. Soren. Simon. Janna. Cole. And Todd, God, please, not Todd. Not any of them!

"And that baby. That fucked-up mongrel has to die."

She froze, gaping at him. Surely he didn't mean little Teddy. Surely no one was sadistic enough to want a child dead?

His eyes were cold and calculating, telling her he was.

Not the baby. God, not the baby.

Todd! her soul screamed, desperate for a connection with someone. Desperate to warn him so he could warn the others.

"You shouldn't have gotten mixed up with that dirty Voss clan." Emmett shook his head.

"What are you talking about?"

"They shouldn't have crossed species lines!" he roared.

Anna rocked back on her heels.

"Leave her alone!" the young woman screamed.

"The hell I will!" Emmett yelled, turning purple with rage. "This is just what Victor worked so hard to stamp out."

Anna shook her head. Who the hell was Victor?

Emmett's tirade went on. "Bears mixing with wolves. Wolves mixing with humans. They dilute the bloodlines. They weaken us all!"

Anna shook her head. God, he really was nuts.

"Victor was just as crazy as you are!" the young woman yelled back.

"You'll see," he snarled back. "Someday, shifters of all species will thank us for our work."

Shifters? A memory from the furthest reaches of her mind stirred. Bears...wolves... Like the stories Sarah had once told her about. Of men who could change shapes from human to animal. Of animals who could shed their skins and walk on two feet. It sounded so romantic at the time, but even as kids, they'd known the idea of shifters was ridiculous.

This man didn't seem to think it was ridiculous. But clearly, he was out of his mind.

She turned the golf club in her hands, searching for a better grip. Where should she aim when he advanced? His head? His knees? His ribs?

"Run." The young woman nodded for the hills. "Run!"

"Yeah," Emmett said, grinning wickedly. "Run. That would make this more fun."

He stepped forward slowly, motioning for the hills. God, he really meant it. He wanted to chase her down.

Todd! she screamed inside in spite of herself. There was no way Todd could hear her. There was no way he could help.

So help yourself, damn it! the other side of her mind yelled back.

"Go ahead. Run." Emmett encouraged her with a wave.

She steeled her nerves and made the quickest, craziest plan of her life. The truck was her best way out, but to get to it, she had to get past Emmett. The only other way out was through thick scrub. But that would never work. She could already feel the thorns tearing at her skin and clothes.

Emmett grinned wider, and his teeth looked longer and pointier than before.

"Catch me," she blurted, then turned and sprinted for the hills.

Chapter Fifteen

Anna knew she had only one chance to pull this off.

She ran, imagining little Teddy. Sarah. Soren. Todd. She had to get this exactly right. She had to get away from this lunatic and warn the others of his awful plan.

Behind her, Emmett cackled in glee and broke into a run.

Chase me, you bastard, she wanted to shout. *Chase me.*

Heavy footsteps thumped the soil behind her. In two more steps, she'd reach the thick scrub where it would be impossible to run at full speed.

Right there. She focused on a low, flat rock that lay at the edge of the clearing. That was her spot.

Something whipped through the space around her hair — Emmett grasping for her.

"Run," he snickered. "Run."

Oh, she'd run all right. Just not where he expected her to. She stretched her legs and made her next step a leap aimed at the rock.

The second her left foot hit the surface, she planted her right foot and whirled, swinging the club like a bat.

Swing from the hips, she remembered her dad coaching her through softball. *You get more power that way.*

She swung her hips, followed through with her shoulders, then gaped as the golf club whacked into Emmett's head with a sickening crack.

Emmett's eyes widened the split second before the golf club struck his temple. He yelped — too late to dodge it — and crumpled to the ground.

She stared for a moment, sick to her stomach, then hurried to the woman and pulled at the rope.

"Go!" the woman told her. "Just go!"

She scratched at the ropes, but the worn fiber refused to slide loose.

"Go! You have to save them!" the woman cried.

"I can get it." She tore with her nails, working at the ends. Emmett groaned and stirred.

"Go!"

Every instinct told her to help this woman, but Emmett was slowly swaying to his feet.

"You bitch," he said in a pained growl.

"Run!"

The young woman's words spurred Anna into motion. She sprinted down the footpath around the boulder, desperately calculating her next moves. She'd left the truck unlocked. The key was in her pocket. She had to get in and lock the doors manually, then pull out the key.

Emmett cursed behind her. His boots thudded over rock.

She hammered as fast over the ground as she could. She'd get the key out and drive like a banshee. Then she'd try the phone until she got a hold of someone to come help. Some helpful hikers, maybe, or the police. Then—

She leaned into the bend, shot around the boulder, and screeched to a sudden stop.

Six men formed a wall in front of her, daring her to break through.

Help! She wanted to grab their arms and gesture behind her. *There's a crazy man who's tied up a woman. He wants to kill me and—*

Part of her mind continued composing the plea for help, but a sinking sensation in her gut told her there was no use. Those men were not hikers, and they were certainly not the police.

She sidestepped, putting her back to the story-high boulder as Emmett came teetering into view.

"Get her," Emmett barked, and they all closed in.

She backed up, panting wildly. Jesus, Emmett had a whole band of thugs to back him up. How could she get away? Could she scramble up the rocks? Swing again and hope for a miracle? Drop to her knees and plead?

"But don't kill her," Emmett added. "Yet."

Her stomach lurched.

"I need to teach her a lesson first," he finished, flashing a toothy grin.

She scratched the idea of dropping to her knees. Which left climbing the rock or trying to take down six men — seven, counting Emmett — with one golf club. A glance over her shoulder showed a smooth sheet of rock that stretched over her head. No way to get a foothold.

Fight. You have to stand and fight.

She tightened her hands on the club and tried to think of some other way out. Short of flying, however, she couldn't come up with anything.

She scooted two steps right to where the boulder curved inward, giving her some protection from the sides. But Jesus, it wasn't going to be enough. Even if she could fight these men one at a time, all they had to do was tire her out and grab their chance.

"Purity. Purity." The men started chanting as they closed in on her.

Her throat went dry, imagining her own death. A slow, painful one at the hands of lunatics. What would happen to the other woman? Would they kill her, too?

One of the men stepped forward, and she shoved everything from her mind except the image of little Teddy. Somehow, she had to hold out until help came. If she died here, these lunatics could lure the others out the way they'd tricked her and kill them one by one.

"Purity," the closest man chanted. His eyes darted around, looking for an opening in her defense.

She swung the golf club right. Just the move he was looking for, because he reached to intercept the shaft.

"Wrong," she murmured, changing direction and swung the club high, then brought it crashing down toward his head.

The man threw his arms that way fast enough to deflect the blow from his head to his shoulder, but the club still connected with a heavy thump.

He grunted and fell back, clutching his shoulder.

"You idiot," Emmett barked. "How hard can it be?"

She refrained from pointing to the lump on Emmett's head and brought the golf club to a ready position instead.

Two men exchanged glances, nodded, and came for her.

"Over here," one of them goaded her.

"Over here," the other echoed, snapping his fingers for her attention.

What was she, a rabid dog backed into a corner?

Well, she sure wasn't far off.

She was so desperate, she grabbed on to the notion and decided to run with it. She channeled rabid-dog vibes and bared her teeth. Why the hell not?

"Over here," she shot back, wiggling the end of the golf club. The sun glinted off the head, making the man on the right squint.

There, her inner coach yelled, and she swung. A short, karate chop that caught the man on the arm and pushed him back, leaving her a fraction of a second to backhand the second man. He warded off the blow, taking the brunt of the force with his forearm, and she swore she heard the bone crack. He was still reaching for her with his left hand, though, and she had just enough time for a defensive jab. It was aimed at his face, and though it landed on his collarbone, she still counted that as her point.

Another crack, another cry of pain.

Anna gulped back the bile in her throat and found her footing as the two men fell back. Two others took their place.

"Shift!" Emmett screamed at them. "Go for her throat."

The men paused and considered for a moment, then nodded as the others chanted away.

"Purity. Purity."

"What kind of men are you?" she screamed, desperate for one of them to come to his senses and call off the attack. "What kind of cowards?"

The two closest to her squared their shoulders and let their jaws hang open.

"Not men," Emmett sneered. "Shifters."

One of the men made a choking sound and doubled over. The other bared his teeth. Anna stared, unable to tear her gaze from the flash of white. The *lengthening* flash of white.

"What the. . . ?"

"Shifters," Emmett repeated as the man pulled his lips back farther.

She wasn't imagining things. His canines *were* getting longer.

"The last of the chosen few," Emmett went on. "Those committed to preserving our bloodlines."

She gasped aloud as hair broke out all over the closest man's skin.

"There are those who wish to stop us, but we will stop them. We will stop all of you."

The closest man fell to all fours. His shirt split down his back. Beside him, the second man shook off scraps of fabric, revealing a curved back covered in hair.

"Wolf. . ." she stuttered. Good God, the men were changing into beasts.

She dared glancing away just long enough to stare at Emmett. He stood on two feet, utterly unchanged, grinning at her.

The scar. Look at the scar. She focused on the scar running straight up from one lip. *Same scar as the wolf who came running out of the woods the day of her hike.*

She stared at Emmett and read the truth in his eyes. Shifter. Man. Wolf.

"Jesus." She looked back at the wolves that stood before her. One shook his coat as if coming in from the rain, and the other flicked his tail and showed his teeth.

"You see?" Emmett cackled as the beasts growled. "Wolves belong with wolves, and bears belong with bears."

Her mind spun. If these guys were the wolves, who were the bears?

141

"Humans belong with humans." He pointed at her. "And you have dared to cross species lines. Don't you see?"

She didn't see anything but the loathing in his eyes.

"You are unpure," he said, practically spitting the words out.

She swung the golf club, warning away the wolves while her mind picked the riddle apart.

You've whored yourself to that bear, Emmett had said.

She hadn't whored herself to anyone, but yes, she had slept with Todd.

"You must die," Emmett concluded, clapping his hands.

The two wolves snarled and stepped forward.

Bear... Todd...

Stop thinking! Just act!

She dropped the threads of thought that had started to connect *Todd* and *bear* and wound up for another swing.

It made her sick, how easy she found it to strike out at an enemy and hope for blood, even death. She'd never killed anything but insects in her life. But suddenly, she was thrust into the role of warrior in a fight to the death. And her death was only part of a greater scheme. Worse still was the idea of someone as innocent as little Teddy dying.

Teddy, Todd's son.

The idea fueled her in a way muscle alone never would have done, and while everything at the edges of her vision blurred, the center was frighteningly clear. She focused on the wolves before her.

Kill them. Kill them now.

Metal shone in a wide arc as she unleashed a furious blow. She struck the wolf on the right on the shoulder. The other leaped forward with a growl, and she punched it back with a jab at the nose.

They both backed up, shook their dark coats, and closed in again. The four men behind them chanted their eerie chant, and Emmett LeBlanc cheered it all on.

Part of her watched like an out-of-body experience. How on earth was she going to overcome these odds?

The wolves sprang forward in tandem, tearing at her legs, and she jumped back, raking the space before her with the golf club. One of the wolves went sprawling but the other dashed forward, and she kicked just in time to connect with its muzzle.

She swung the golf club back to a ready position, panting wildly.

"Get her!" Emmett yelled.

Another attack; another blur. She hacked and swung and chopped until her shoulders ached. She swung too wide, slamming her weapon into the boulder, and the blow vibrated right into her arms. Then it wasn't only wolf jaws snapping at her, but human hands, too. The other men had joined in, crowding her tiny space.

"No!" she screamed when one caught the golf club and wrenched it out of her hands.

She kicked at one wolf, but another dove in, butting her legs. She teetered, clawing desperately at the hands reaching for her, but it was too late. She fell, but the man hauled her to her feet and slapped her so hard, her vision went double for a moment.

A moment too long, because two blurry Emmetts moved in and four greedy hands reached out.

"Gotcha, bitch!"

Emmett grabbed her by the neck and gripped hard, squeezing the life out of her.

"You see?" he screamed in triumph.

She clawed at his face and arms, desperate to get free.

"Thought you could fight with me, little bitch?"

She landed a kick at his shins, and his grip loosened just long enough for her to suck in a breath of air.

"Don't make this harder on yourself, honey."

She scratched at his eyes, but she could barely see. Her kicks grew weaker, and she wheezed desperately. God, she couldn't breathe.

"You will die, and the others, too." Emmett's face was purple with rage, and his stale breath stuck in her nose.

She closed her eyes, unable to face him any more. If she had to die, she'd shut her mind off to the worst of it.

Don't die! Fight him! an inner voice cried.

She gave another weak kick, a feeble punch, but he parried both easily.

Don't die. Hang in there.

She knew she had to be dying, because the voice no longer sounded like her own. It came whispering into her mind from a distance, like an angel in her hour of need.

She allowed herself a tiny inner smile. That's what she'd think of. An angel.

The funny thing was, she'd always pictured angels as women with fluttery white gowns and wings, but the image that came to her was of Todd.

Don't die. Not now. Not like this.

Why did the words sound so familiar?

"You see?" Emmett raged on, but his voice grew fainter. "No one can stop us."

Don't die. The angel's voice grew fainter.

How could she not die? She didn't have any air.

Emmett changed his grip on her throat, and she gulped a tiny breath of air.

Not now. Not like this.

Maybe the angel was right. Maybe she could last a little longer.

Why bother? part of her wailed, ready for it to be over.

Hang on. Just hang on, the angel pleaded in her mind.

She stopped struggling and tried anticipating Emmett's shakes. He rattled her back and forth like a rag doll, making her sick. But when he pushed her body away from his, his fingers let up a little, and if she was quick enough, she could catch a little air.

"Say it!" Emmett screamed on. "Tell me I was right!"

Hold on...

She tried to, but the world was getting darker. Even with her eyes closed, she could feel her awareness slip away.

"Tell me I am the best—"

Emmett's tirade was cut off by a mighty roar that ripped out of nowhere, and the ground shook under her feet. The earth seemed to swallow her up, and she crashed into something hard.

Breathe, the angel ordered as the world around her exploded in barks and growls.

She blinked, finding herself on the ground, fallen in a heap.

"You," Emmett cried in a disbelieving voice.

Anna managed to roll sideways, away from the chaos just inches from her side. She twisted to a belly-down position and gasped wildly.

Alive. She was alive.

Dust flew through the air, choking her. She pushed to her knees, then her feet, leaning heavily against the boulder. That side of her universe was safe. The other was a tornado. A typhoon. A battlefield.

"Get him! Get him!" Emmett yelled.

A deep, furious bellow replied, followed by a heavy thump.

She blinked frantically. What was happening?

Sun glinted off steel, and she spotted the golf club at her feet. She nearly lost her balance reaching for it, but her fingers closed around the handle and whipped it back just before a massive paw stepped into that space.

A massive, furry paw connected to a thickly muscled leg.

She fell back against the boulder, gaping upward.

A bear. A grizzly bear?

It was on its back legs, and fur bristled all over its back. Thick and shiny, the bear's coat shook with each of his furious roars.

She shrank back against the rock, trembling.

The bear made a barrier in front of her, crowding her space. Beyond it, a dozen smaller paws shuffled left and right, and a chorus of growls met each of the bear's roars.

Clutching the golf club, she pushed herself back to her feet and stared. The bear was fighting the wolves off. He was helping her.

"Every Voss will die!" Emmett screamed.

Voss? Todd was a Voss. Soren was a Voss, and Simon was, too.

The threads her mind had been trying to weave together earlier started connecting again.

You've whored yourself to that bear. . .

The dipper is his nose, Todd had said, showing her the stars. *It's a grizzly, not a polar bear.*

Shifters, Emmett had sneered. *And you have dared cross species lines.*

Species, as in humans and bears.

The bear bellowed again, and she stared.

Todd was a bear?

A bear— he'd started saying about Teddy before he corrected it to baby. *A baby needs other things, too.*

The baby is going to be the first to die, Emmett had said.

The baby was a bear? A shifter?

Her startled mind flew back to their conversation under the stars.

How does the bear know it's his mate? she'd asked, thinking it was all make-believe.

He knows the second he sees her. That's the easy part.

She remembered the moment she'd laid eyes on him at the door to the saloon the first time they'd met. How strong the pull was even then, how hard it was to see him hurry by.

The hard part is making sure he's worthy of her, Todd had explained in a choked voice.

A teary cry broke from her throat, and the bear glanced back.

"Todd," she whispered, staring into his impossibly blue eyes.

He chuffed, and it was a mournful sound. Then he turned back to their attackers and swung a paw spiked with four-inch claws.

Todd. Claws. Paws.

Holy shit.

Anna took a deep breath and dried the handle of the golf club with her shirt. Every movement seemed too slow, like her mind, but she had a grasp of the basics at last. Wolves, bad. Bear, good. Fight to the death.

And damn it, she was not going to die.

Her mind zoomed from the biggest overview to the tiniest details, like the fact that her hands were all sweaty, and she needed a good grip if she wanted to help Todd fight the wolves off.

"They want to kill everyone. Teddy, too," she cried.

The bear bellowed and swept forward, going from defense to attack. Wolves snapped at him from all directions, darting in and out, working as a team.

Yeah, well. She could do that, too. Anna stepped forward, holding the golf club up, looking for her chance.

One of the wolves darted forward, focused entirely on the bear. She gripped the golf club with both hands and brought it crashing down between its shoulder blades. The wolf yelped, fell, and then crawled away, whimpering like she ought to feel sorry for it.

As if.

The other wolves bayed in outrage. The bear took another step forward, challenging them.

A challenge that was met instantly. Furiously. The bear — Todd? — took care of most of the assault, but Anna covered his left side enough to let him focus on driving them back. With a mighty swipe of the left paw, he hurtled one wolf aside. It yelped and lay still. The others cut in and out, looking for an opening.

All of the men were in wolf form now, and Anna didn't have to wonder which was Emmett LeBlanc. If the scar hadn't given him away, his commanding yips would have — yips that consistently sounded from the relative safety of the back of the pack.

"Coward," she muttered.

He showed his teeth.

She cut the legs out from under the next wolf who ventured too near, and Todd finished him off with both sets of claws.

Both sets, she noticed. He favored the right paw, but it was just as effective as the left.

Deadly, in other words.

Still, they were one bear and one human against seven determined wolves. Whatever the wolves' misguided mission might be, it drove them to risk their necks again and again.

147

Get them! She could practically hear the order coded into Emmett's snarls.

The wolves hung back for one second then jumped forward at once. Todd lunged forward to meet them while Anna stood a step behind, swinging at the one wolf who seemed assigned to take her on. A smart one that waited for her to swing wide then attempted to dash in. Its teeth clicked together an inch away from her knee, and she stumbled back, landing on her rear.

Todd roared and loomed over the wolf, then reached out with a massive paw and struck. The wolf tumbled before crashing into a rock and going limp.

Deadly limp.

Todd looked at her, and she swore he was about to reach a hand out to pull her to her feet before he realized it was a paw.

"Watch out!" she screamed, pointing to the wolf leaping at him from behind. An incredibly high, incredibly bold leap that Todd turned too late to intercept.

The wolf went for Todd's ear — far from a mortal blow, but still, Anna cried out.

"No!"

She could predict how the wolf wanted it to play out. He'd drag Todd's ear down with his weight. The others would be on top of him in a flash. Even a bear of Todd's size couldn't withstand the weight of several two-hundred-pound wolves.

Todd roared, swiping at the wolf, but it was too late.

Now! Emmett's bark seemed to indicate, and the others closed in.

She saw the whites of Emmett's eyes. The red of Todd's lips. The saliva-covered ivory of several sets of jaws, closing in on him.

She yelled and dashed forward, swinging the golf club wide. Recklessly wide, exposing the front of her body. She had to in order to build the momentum needed to break that attack. She knew nothing about golf and even less about polo, but she'd seen pictures of polo players leaning way out from their ponies to whack the ball, and that's just what she did. She swung it wide while running forward, then arced it forward and—

Whack!

The golf club connected, and the vibration that went through it transmitted the shattering of bone. That wolf yelped and fell while Anna stumbled forward. She fell right toward the next wolf who jumped forward, its jaws opened wide.

Die, those jaws screamed at her. *Now you will die.*

Chapter Sixteen

Duck! came a booming voice.

She ducked, obeying even before she actively processed the word. The voice was that powerful, that sure.

Whoosh! A giant paw — and five killer claws — swiped the air an inch over her head, ripping along the wolf's neck. The counterattack came with a roar that echoed through the canyon and in her ears.

She nearly cheered, but it was too soon. Todd's move had put him off-balance, and another wolf jumped in from the right to take advantage. She barely had the space to backhand it with the club. She spun into her strike, moving away from the bear, creating room for both of them to move.

The bear — Todd — roared in disapproval, obviously preferring her close.

I need space to maneuver, and you do, too. She thought the words rather than speaking them because she was still short of breath.

Need to keep you safe, his grunt told her.

Need to stop these bastards, she thought, gritting her teeth. *They're after Teddy. They're after all of you.*

Todd roared to high heaven and lumbered forward for what she knew was his final attack. The wolves tripped over each other, stumbling in their haste. A few hurried to get away, while others rushed to launch their own counterattacks. A third wolf fell victim to Todd's slashing claws, and then a fourth. Blood flew, and she squinted against the horrifying sight. But she kept up her own blows, too, because she had to.

When there were three wolves left, Todd flew at them, ripping and slashing until one lay dead and another ran for its life. He spun to face the final wolf, who kept his back to the rocks.

Emmett LeBlanc — in wolf form — raised his lips and snarled, but she could see the fear in his eyes.

Todd reared high on his back feet, dwarfing his foe, then crashed forward at exactly the same moment Emmett tried to flee.

Too late.

Anna turned her head, but she couldn't close her eyes to the sickening slashing sounds. The wolf screamed, snarled, and abruptly fell silent.

Then it was quiet but for the heavy pants of the bear. Her breath was choppy too because, Jesus, it was over. Six of the seven wolves were dead. One had fled. She and Todd had survived.

She and Todd. Todd, the bear.

He bellowed in the direction of the wolf who'd fled, then came back down to all fours with a low chuff.

Everything went quiet again — deathly quiet, from the harsh scrublands to the birds that had flown away and even the insects that seemed to have taken cover during the fight. Between one hammering heartbeat and the next, the full scope of what had just transpired caught up with her, and she half fell, half sat on the rocky ground. The golf club clattered off a rock, and she froze when Todd turned.

His right paw was tucked against his body, and she could see the pain in his eyes. But there was triumph in them, too. She could see it in the straight line of his back, the sharp angle of his ears. His muzzle was splashed with blood, as was his shoulder, but he stood at attention like a general on the field of victory.

"We did it," she whispered, staring at him.

His massive bear chin dipped once. Twice.

"You did it," she whispered, correcting herself. He'd done all the work. Jesus, without him, she'd have been long dead.

The bear swung his head left then right in clear disagreement. *We,* he seemed to be saying. *We did it.*

Her throat ached from where LeBlanc had crushed her windpipe, and her left ankle throbbed from a wrenching motion she only vaguely remembered. Her fingers hurt from gripping the golf club so tightly, and when she brushed her cheek, she found blood. Her blood? The enemy's?

She sat staring dumbly at the blood on her hand, as close to the edge of panic as she'd ever been. The fight was over, but it all replayed in her mind, all the more terrifying for the realization of how many near misses she and Todd had survived. Her hands started shaking, her knees knocking, and all she could see was blood.

She was about to hide her face in her hands when a huge, brown muzzle crept closer. Todd moved slowly, holding his breath, and she held hers, too. It didn't seem possible to come that close to a grizzly, just as it didn't seem possible for a beast of that size to have suddenly grown so quiet and gentle.

He chuffed once. *It's okay. Everything is okay.*

Her heart beat faster instead of slowing down, and she closed her eyes, because the bear was coming even closer. Its breath warmed her cheek. She froze, every muscle in her body stiff.

Then something soft and velvety touched down on her cheek. Her heart skipped a beat.

He licked her — the tiniest, most careful lick in bear history, she'd bet — and she giggled. One of those *I'm not sure if I'm about to scream or laugh* kind of giggles that could have gone either way. When Todd licked her again, she caught his muzzle in both hands and held on.

He licked the blood from her cheek, then puffed gently in her ear. That time, she cackled out of sheer relief.

"I'm okay," she whispered, answering the question in his eyes. "Are you okay?"

The top of his tongue showed pink in the T-intersection of bear nose and mouth. *I'm okay.*

Which just about made her melt into the rock behind her until a thought hit her out of the blue.

"Oh, God! We have to check on the girl!" She scrambled to her feet and made for the pathway behind the rock.

Her steps were slow and creaky, like an old woman's, but she plowed on despite Todd's questioning chuffs. The second she trotted out on the other side of the boulders, the young woman cried out in relief. She'd been straining at the end of her bonds, but the moment she saw Anna, her knees gave way.

"Did you...? Are they...?"

Anna rushed forward. "They're gone. Oh, you poor thing," she cried at the blood caked around the young woman's wrists. She worked the ropes as gently as she could, but the thick, rough strands still sawed at the woman's skin.

"Just do it," the woman said through clenched teeth. "Please, just get me free."

Anna glanced over her shoulder. Todd hadn't followed, and she could hear his heavy footsteps thump into the distance. Was he making sure that last wolf wasn't coming back?

"Quickly," the woman begged. "We have to save them."

To Anna, *them* meant Teddy, Sarah, and the others. Who was the woman talking about?

"Emmett forced me to help them." Tears slipped down the stranger's cheeks, but her voice was stubbornly even. "Please believe me."

"I believe you," she assured the girl. The blood on her wrists was proof, just as the worry in her eyes was. "Do you know them? Those... those shifters?"

The word felt foreign on her tongue. Had she really just seen men turn into wolves? Had her lover really beaten them as a bear?

The woman nodded without asking what shifters were. Did that mean she could turn into an animal, too? "My stepfather was one of them," she said. "In the beginning, it wasn't so bad. He was all talk and no action. But then Emmett Whyte started—"

"Emmett LeBlanc," Anna corrected, still working at the ropes.

The woman shook her head. "He used a lot of false names, but he's a Whyte. Brother of the worst one of all. They made me stay with them. I swear I never hurt anyone. But it got worse and worse, and I couldn't get out."

154

"It's okay," Anna said, trying to calm her down. "They're gone now."

"I would never have gone along with it if they hadn't threatened to kill the others."

Finally, the ropes slipped free, and the woman toppled forward.

"What others?" Anna asked, helping her to her feet.

The woman gulped and stumbled down the path, back to the parking lot. "I have to check on them. I have to see if they're all right."

"Who?" Anna asked.

The woman broke into a stiff trot, and Anna followed. Her steps grew faster and faster as she headed for the van at the end of the lot — so fast that Anna could barely keep up. For a moment, she thought the woman had tricked her and was trying to get away. But she headed for the back of the van, not the front, racing for the open doors where she stopped in her tracks. Anna raced after her, terrified that they'd find more wolves — or worse, dead bodies of innocent victims or something equally horrifying.

When she caught up a second later, she pulled up short and stared at what she saw.

The last wolf that had run off lay in a pool of blood two steps away, and inside the van...

Todd. Human Todd, thank God, sitting quietly. His sandy brown hair was disheveled, his chest covered in dust. His eyes flickered to Anna and the woman before he dipped his chin.

"It's okay, little guy," he whispered, cuddling a tiny bear cub to his chest.

Anna stared as the cub made pathetic mewing sounds and buried its face against Todd's shoulder.

"Shh. It will be okay."

"Fay," the woman called anxiously, climbing into the van. There was a bench built into one side, while the rest was an open storage space crowded with boxes and bags. She moved past Todd and reached into a cardboard box. "Oh, my God. Fay, are you okay?"

She pulled a tiny bundle wrapped in a tattered, rose-colored blanket from the box and held it close. Anna caught sight of a bare foot — a teensy, tiny, human foot with five toes — and gasped.

"A baby?"

The baby made a little choking sound then cried. And cried and cried as tears streamed down the young woman's face.

Anna gaped at Todd. "How did you know they were in here?"

He shrugged. "I heard them."

She stared at his nonchalance. She hadn't heard anything. "Wow."

Wow to everything. Todd could turn into a bear, and he wasn't the only one. Which made her wonder. Was the cub a shifter, too? What about the baby girl?

"Emmett and the others killed their parents. A bear and a cougar shifter," the young woman said in answer to her unspoken question. "They were going to kill the babies, too. I tried everything I could to stop them." She rocked back and forth, trying to soothe herself, perhaps, as much as the child. "I said we could keep them for ransom and bait some other shifters out with them. And God, I was so scared they would try it." She clutched the baby close as it wailed on.

"Did they?" Todd asked. His voice was hard and edgy, like the bear might jump out of him any second.

"No. Not yet. They kept the cubs alive until now, but I think they were starting to have second thoughts. I was so scared they would kill them..."

She sobbed and shook and looked up at Anna with desperate eyes. "Please." She held the baby out. "Please, help me. I try everything I can, but she cries a lot. I've been trying to get her to eat, but Emmett wouldn't let me get formula, just milk. She's been losing weight and getting weaker. Please."

The second Anna slid into the seat beside her, the young woman handed over the baby and doubled over her knees, crying.

Anna held the baby close with one hand and patted the young woman with the other. "It's okay. You did your best.

You saved them."

"But she's getting so weak..." The woman's voice was desperate, afraid. "And Ben." She looked toward the cub in Todd's arms. "I've never seen a shifter baby change forms that young. But he was so scared, it just happened, and I haven't been able to get him to shift back."

"You can stay a bear for a while," Todd whispered into the cub's ear. "It's okay. Everything is going to be okay."

He was talking to the cub, but Anna's heart rate slowed down a tick at the reassurance in his voice.

"What's your name?" she asked the young woman.

"Summer."

"I think they're going to be okay."

The baby was quieting down already, staring up at Anna with yellow-green eyes. Her breath caught in her throat, and she couldn't drag her eyes away. She looked and looked and looked, and it reminded her of the way she'd first passed Todd in the saloon doors. Something shifted inside her, and this time, she recognized the feeling.

It was her soul announcing, *This one is mine. This one belongs to me.*

The man. And now, the baby. She took a deep breath. Was this really happening?

She held the baby closer, and the tiny eyes blinked. *Are you a good wolf or a bad wolf?* they seemed to ask.

Anna shook her head and whispered, "I'm not a wolf at all."

"You sure fight like one," Summer murmured.

Anna sat a little straighter. "I'm not a bear, either." She glanced at Todd, wondering what he would say. "I'm just me."

That's all I want, his eyes said. *All I need.*

She looked down at the baby. "But I'll do everything I can to help you, sweet little thing."

The baby seemed content with that and gripped Anna's pinkie in her tiny little fist.

"Wow," Anna breathed, looking at her.

"I don't know what to do," Summer cried, tossing up her hands. "They don't have anyone."

Todd made a gruff sound that sounded a lot like, *They do now.*

"I don't know anything about babies," Summer went on, overwhelmed.

Anna didn't, either, but something deep inside her promised she would figure it out fast.

"Doesn't take much," Todd said, petting the cub between its ears. "A little feeding, a lot of holding. A lot of love."

It looked like it would take ten men with a crowbar to pry that cub out of his arms. Anna smiled.

The sun was just starting to set outside, and the light filtering through the back of the van was a soft orange-pink. It backlit Todd's body and streamed in around the bundle in his arms. During the fight, everything had been harsh desert tones, but now, everything had calmed to a warm, comforting glow.

"We got this," Todd whispered to the cub. "Don't you worry, little guy."

Then he looked at her, and she smiled. It seemed crazy to feel so calm in such a crazy situation, but she was. Calm and serene.

She nodded at Todd, then looked down at the baby girl in her arms. "We got this."

Chapter Seventeen

Todd lost track of time. He got lost in the softness of the tiny cub's ears and in the presence of Anna nearby. Jesus, what a woman. She'd just had the reality of shifters introduced to her in the worst possible way, and yet she hadn't fled for the hills. When she looked at him, it wasn't in disgust or horror. She just smiled.

But when the engine of an approaching car sounded outside, she clutched the baby and paled. "Are they back?"

The cub panicked, too, sinking its claws into Todd's arm and burrowing against his chest.

He murmured to the cub. No, the rogue wolves weren't back, and thank God for that. Footsteps sounded, and Soren's face appeared at the open door of the van. The second he peered in, he did a double take.

"Holy shit." Soren's eyes darted between Anna, him, the young woman, and the babies. "I mean, shoot," he added, shooting an apologetic look at the babies.

Todd would have given a million bucks for a camera to catch the look on his cousin's face. No, wait. He would have given a million bucks to go back in time and capture a time-lapse sequence of Anna's face. The initial shock, then the wonder. The hope. The love, already pouring out toward the babies and at him.

At *him*. A messed-up bear.

At some point, she'd just grinned, and he had the feeling she'd been playing with her own mental camera, too. Aiming it his way and nodding in satisfaction until all his worries about being worthy gradually faded away.

Mate, his bear hummed.

No doubt about it. Anna's scream for help had sounded in his mind miles away when he'd gone to check the scent Zack had found. No one else heard it — just him — and he'd raced for his mate with a speed and fury not even the fleetest wolf could match.

"Yeah," he nodded wearily. "Holy shit."

The cub fit in the scoop of his arm, and he flexed and straightened the fingers of his injured hand. They had worked when he needed them to. Everything had worked. Maybe he wasn't a complete washout, after all.

"Oh, my God," Sarah said, appearing beside her mate. "What happened?"

That was the million-dollar question, and he wasn't really sure he had the answer.

Soren, though, took one sniff of the scene of the attack and growled. "The Blue Bloods." He all but spat the name.

"Blue Bloods?" Anna asked in a shaky voice.

Everyone looked at her, then at the young woman hunched in the back of the van.

Little by little, it all came out once they were back in the saloon, where the stranger — Summer — explained what had happened. Emmett Whyte — aka Emmett LeBlanc — had been hunting down Sarah for months, while his cronies, the last of the Blue Bloods, had been on their own mission to wipe out any shifters who dared cross species lines.

Ty, Tina, Lana, and several other Twin Moon wolves had rushed over to the saloon, too, and they all hung on the young woman's words.

"I knew it wasn't Roy," Ty growled.

"Shh," Lana chided. "Let her speak."

"I was there the day they got word of Victor Whyte's death," Summer explained in a shaky voice. "I thought that was it — that they'd finally give up. But instead, they decided to keep up what they called the crusade. They targeted packless couples in remote places." She buried her face in her hands. "They started talking about going after babies."

Soren had growled audibly at that, and Sarah shrank back with a look of horror.

160

"I swear I didn't want anything to do with any of it." When Summer looked up, her face was streaked with tears. "I talked them into keeping the twins alive, but that only made them concoct worse plans. Like coming after other couples and other babies." She looked at Sarah, who turned away, instinctively shielding little Teddy. "They wanted to use Anna to lure you out next."

"Jesus," Soren muttered, looking at his mate. His face was red, his fists clenched. Then he swallowed hard and looked Todd in the eye.

I owe you, man. I owe you everything.

Todd sucked in a deep breath. He'd always lived to serve, knowing that the reward would be an ephemeral thing. But that look, that scratchy tone in his cousin's voice said it all.

You done good, man. You done good.

"Are you sure they were the last ones?" Sarah asked. "Are you sure?"

"I think so."

"You *think* so?" Soren roared.

Todd was about to step forward and glare at his cousin, but Anna beat him to it. Anna, who'd fought off half a dozen wolves and taken in two babies unquestioningly, because she was all heart. Anna, who was still on her feet after a hell of a day, because she was that tough.

"She did what she could. Don't you see that?"

Sarah put a hand on Soren's arm, and Todd could hear the thoughts passing between the two of them. *She's, what? Twenty-three, twenty-four? What else could she do?*

"I'm not sure if there are any others," Summer sniffled, hugging herself. Then she looked up, shaken to the core but determined to meet the eyes of not one, but two angry alphas — Soren and Ty — to show that she was telling the truth.

God, was she tough, too. Almost as tough as his amazing mate.

"I'm sorry." She shook her head. "I can't be sure."

Todd stepped between her and the others. *She's been through enough.*

161

Ty nodded slowly then looked at the babies. "Bear-cougar cubs, huh? We need to find them a good home."

Jessica grinned, looking between Todd and Anna. "I think fate already has."

Todd gulped, looking at the cub who'd fallen into a fitful sleep in his arms. Jessica had tried prying the little guy away from him, but the tiny bear had only snuggled closer to his chest. And though it scared Todd like nothing ever had before — the responsibility, the risks — the choice had been an easy one.

"I don't think it was fate doing the deciding." Tina Hawthorne smiled.

He gulped, because what exactly did you say to that? Especially when it was true. Fate had just about shouted into his head that moment he'd first held the cub.

Once again, warrior, I give you my most precious gift. A gift I rarely bestow once, let alone twice. A reward reserved only for the bravest, most loyal heroes. I award you a choice. The chance to steer your own destiny. So choose, and choose well.

He stood perfectly still, though every nerve in his body hummed like a high-tension wire. The first choice, back when he'd lain dying in the animal shelter, had been simpler because it was all about him, and all there was at stake was his body. This time, it was about his heart and about innocent lives that depended on him.

Choose, warrior, fate boomed again.

Fate hadn't been fucking with him all along. It had offered him a choice, tested him sorely, and then rewarded him with a second choice.

And this time, it was a choice of the heart. Was he ready to risk that, too? To truly live and love and take everything that went along with that?

Then Anna had looked over at him, and the choice was an easy one.

So, yes, he'd made his choice, and Anna had made hers the minute she'd nodded to him in the back of the van. *We got this.*

"They're ours," he said to those gathered in the back of the saloon. Loud and clear, in case fate was wondering if he would change his mind.

As if.

He looked over at Anna. Jesus, she barely knew what she was getting herself into. Was it fair to ask her to decide something so important based on so little? To take such a leap of faith?

Her eyes shone as she looked at him, full of faith and resolve, and she nodded.

"They're ours," she whispered, keeping her eyes on his.

So, yeah, it was decided. But boy did he have a hell of a lot of explaining to do.

∞∞∞

The funny thing was, things went pretty smoothly after that. They were so busy getting the hang of taking care of the kids that the shifter part came in little bits, and Sarah and the others helped with that, too. A week passed, and then another, and though little Ben still hadn't come out of bear form, the fear gradually faded from his eyes, and he was as content as a little cub should be as long as Todd was around.

"Definitely a daddy's boy." Anna smiled.

Todd had done a double take when she said that. Daddy. Did she really mean him?

He glanced down at the cub snoozing in his arms and thought about all the diapers he'd changed in the last few days.

Daddy. That did have a nice ring to it.

Fay slept half as much and moved twice as quickly as Ben. She had wispy blond hair and striking, yellow-green eyes that were going to halt dozens of men in their tracks someday. At times, they sparkled with curiosity; at others, with mischief. And even though she was only a tiny little thing, she was already wiggling and turning and doing her damnedest to skip crawling altogether and go right to walking, or better yet, running.

"Gonna have a real firecracker on your hands there, man," Soren had joked.

When Ty Hawthorne's old Aunt Jean came over to visit, she'd smiled from ear to ear as she bounced the baby girl on her knee. "A beautiful, healthy little cougar shifter. All energy. All curiosity."

He'd fully expected Anna to go pale at that comment — because, Jesus, wasn't it enough to learn about bears for starters? But she'd just taken Fay back and nuzzled her with her nose. "Healthy and happy. A good start. Right, sweetie?"

The four of them had crowded into the little apartment above the garage with the babies in one room and Anna and him in the other. In the few quiet times they got, Anna asked a lot of questions, and what he couldn't find a way to explain, Sarah, Jessica, and Janna did, thank God. Anna had made him shift back and forth a few times, and slowly, she'd gone from wide-eyed to inquisitive and even delighted. She'd petted his fur, rubbed his ears, and laughed at his tail.

"I can't believe it," she chuckled. "I'm in love with a man who has a tail."

"My bear's the one with a tail," he'd growled.

"My bear," she corrected immediately.

Her bear. He'd been going to sleep each night floating away on those words.

Which made it torture not to give her the mating bite the couple of times they'd had the chance to be alone. The first night back at the apartment over the garage, all they'd done was hang on to each other and stare wordlessly into each other's eyes. But on the second night, after they'd gotten the kids to bed, they'd stripped and went at it like a couple of animals. A couple of breathlessly quiet animals, hoping the cubs wouldn't stir. On the third night, they were too exhausted to do anything except nuzzle, but when they'd risen the next morning, the kids had slept long enough to let them take it slow and sweet.

"What does the bear do when he finds his mate?" she'd whispered to him afterward.

You mean, other than worship her for the rest of his life?
he'd nearly said.

He cleared his throat and chose his words carefully. "When she's ready, he marks her as his. And she marks him the same way."

"How?"

That was the tricky part, because how could he ever explain the concept of a mating bite in a way that wouldn't make a human blanch?

Luckily, Anna continued her question before he could speak. Her voice dropped and her eyes fluttered. "With a mating bite?"

Apparently, Sarah and the other women had briefed her on that, too. And dang, they must have really explained it well — the incredible high, the burning burst of passion that came with a bite delivered at the height of sex that all mated shifters raved about — because Anna looked like she wouldn't mind trying it out for herself.

He'd kissed the curve of her neck, then raked his teeth against her skin, testing her out. Every time he did it, her body rose against his, and the heat between them built to unstoppable levels again. But he'd held back. It had taken everything he had, but he'd managed somehow.

"We have time," he'd whispered. Much as he'd love to roam in the woods with his gorgeous mate in bear form, he figured that turning into a bear was one adjustment Anna had better put off a little while.

"A lifetime," she'd whispered back.

So Anna was in. All in. With him, with the kids. It was crazy, the way fate worked.

"So," she'd said next, looking around the tiny apartment. "We'll need our own place."

He nodded. Space. A reliable income. A safe home for the kids. That's what they needed. But where?

"Montana." Anna said it before he did. "How about Montana?"

Yes, there were a lot of ghosts in Montana, but there were a lot of good memories, too.

Soren, Sarah, and the others all but begged them to stay and help run the saloon, but Anna was just as excited at the prospect of Montana as he was. She could find work just about anywhere, and there was nothing tying her to Virginia any more.

"You're really sure?" Soren asked on the day they were all set to leave. Anna's little hatchback was stuffed with baby gifts and hand-me-downs, and everyone was gathered around to say good-bye. "You're welcome to stay," Soren offered for the tenth time in two weeks.

Todd shifted Ben in his arms and looked the cub in the eyes. They were clear and brown — and sleepy, too. The little guy yawned, showing his pink tongue and tiny milk teeth. Todd rubbed him between the ears.

"Yeah. I'm sure."

Arizona was okay, but Montana was home, and it would be better for the kids, too. More space, more privacy. There was a possibility that Ben might never come out of bear form, and it would be easier to bring him up on a remote mountain property than in the middle of a town.

"You're really sure?" Sarah looked at Anna.

Anna nodded. "Never been so sure of anything in my life."

Good thing bears couldn't explode from joy — or sheer relief.

Soren looked concerned, but he nodded slowly. Safety was his main concern, and Todd's, too. But a couple of bear cousins from the East Coast were keen to come out and help him get the Black River lumber mill running again, along with a few other shifters who'd contacted Twin Moon Ranch for help after the spate of Blue Blood attacks. They were ready for a new start, too, and that brought their numbers to twenty.

A ragtag group of twenty, led by him.

Him, alpha of a whole new clan.

He took a deep breath and nodded at Soren. They'd never let down their guard, but it was time to go home and live without fear again.

"Can I hold them one more time?" Summer asked. She'd spent the past two weeks helping everywhere and working herself to the bone in a desperate effort to prove her distaste for the Blue Bloods. When Soren offered her work in the café and saloon, she'd jumped at the chance, ready to build a new life among the bears and wolves of the Blue Moon Saloon.

Sliding little Ben into Summer's arms left his empty, so Todd took a deep breath and turned to Sarah, who was holding Teddy.

"I need to say good-bye, too," he said.

Sarah bit her lip and nodded slowly. Yeah, they both knew Teddy was going to scream — he always did when Todd came close — but Todd had to hold him one time. Just this one time and then good-bye.

He took little Teddy as carefully as he might handle a crystal vase, tucked him gently up against his shoulder, and closed his eyes. He took a deep breath, pulled together all the love he'd ever felt in his life — from his parents, his cousins, his sweet old grandma, and yes, even his grouchy cousin Soren — and pushed them gently into the baby's mind.

All that love, Teddy. It's all yours. You might not be mine, but a big part of the love is.

He braced himself for the baby's wail. But surprise, surprise — it didn't come. Little Teddy just looked up with big, trusting eyes, tightened his tiny little fingers around Todd's pinkie, and hung on.

Todd held his breath and slowly hugged the child closer. He put his chin on the baby's head and counted every miraculous second that passed. One. Two. Three. Then he took a deep breath, kissed the baby, and handed him back.

"Here you go. Back to Daddy." When he whispered the words, his voice cracked, mirroring the scars on his heart. But some scars were good ones. Some scars, you wore with pride.

Soren locked eyes with him — eyes that were hard to meet, they were so full of emotion. Relief. Gratitude.

And respect. Sweet, sweet, bottomless respect.

Anna put a hand on his shoulder, checking if he was okay.

Well, yes and no. Letting Teddy go made his heart ache, but it felt good, too. To wrap up one thing before launching into another.

"Hey," she whispered. "Someone else needs you."

He turned just in time for her to pop Fay into his arms.

"Hey, who's my girl?" he asked, swooping her up high.

Fay squeaked with joy and kicked at thin air, showing off her strength.

Just as quickly as he'd lifted her up, he dipped her down and smothered her with a smooch that made a ridiculous amount of noise. Well, he figured it did, anyway. Some things, you didn't need to hear to know they were there. Kind of like the *I love you* in his mate's eyes, or the *You done good, man* in his cousin's squared jaw.

Fay grinned her adorable, toothless smile, and Ben mewed for his attention, which meant that Anna was the one who had to pack the last of their bags into her overstuffed hatchback. Finally, she waved the keys in the air.

"I guess that's it."

She hugged everyone in turn — Jessica, Janna, Simon, Cole, Summer, and even Soren, who blushed. Then she stood in front of Sarah and took her cousin by both hands. Both of them looked about to burst out crying, though neither could summon any words. They finally broke into a huge, rocking hug that said it all.

"Promise to visit soon," Sarah whispered at last.

Anna's face glittered with tears, and Todd had to swallow away a lump in his throat, too.

"We will. But you have to visit us, too."

Todd looked at Soren, who nodded solemnly. *You bet we will, man. You bet we will.*

He looked at Anna. Time to go before he started shedding tears — or worse, before Soren did, because he'd never seen his cousin come that close. They maneuvered the kids into their car seats, took one last look around, and got in, ready to drive.

"Bye!" Everyone waved, turning the view outside the windshield into a blur.

Anna tooted the horn, and he stuck a hand out the window to wave back.

They both looked in the rearview mirror as the car swung around a corner and the saloon disappeared from view.

He took a deep breath and squeezed Anna's hand as they navigated out of town, heading for the northbound highway. "Whoa."

She nodded and wiped her glistening cheek with the back of one hand. "Whoa. You know what I'm thinking?"

Her voice was shaky, but hopeful, too.

"What?"

"Mountain meadows in the spring."

He broke into a grin so wide, it hurt and filled in the next part. "Cool, clear summer creeks."

"Berries growing thick in the fall."

He pulled her hand closer and kissed her knuckles.

"Home," he finished.

She nodded and glanced back at the kids. "The funny thing is, I already feel like I'm home."

He turned and looked in the baby mirrors they'd set up. Ben had snoozed off, and Fay was babbling at her toes. Then he reached over and gently twirled a finger in his mate's silky hair.

"I know what you mean. I know what you mean."

Sneak Peek: Deception

On an undercover mission into a den of enemy wolves, there's nothing more dangerous than forbidden love.
She-wolf Summer Smith is desperate to make up for a past she can't deny — and the best way to accomplish that is to take on a deadly mission for her new pack. She'll sacrifice anything to clear her name and protect the people she loves. With the future of shifters across the Southwest resting in her hands, it's the worst possible time to fall in love — with a bear, no less.

Burly bear shifter Drew Kovacs hasn't traveled to the Southwest to look for trouble, and he sure isn't looking for love. But the second he lays eyes on the she-wolf with a mesmerizing smile and haunted eyes, he knows she's the one. There's just one problem — Summer is about to plunge head-first into danger, and he sure as hell won't let her go alone. But he can't show up and blow her undercover mission, either. Unless. . .

Don't miss the passion, suspense,, or romance. Get your copy of DECEPTION today! Available as ebook, paperback, and audiobook.

Books by Anna Lowe

Blue Moon Saloon

Perfection (a short story prequel)

Damnation (Book 1)

Temptation (Book 2)

Redemption (Book 3)

Salvation (Book 4)

Deception (Book 5)

Celebration (a holiday treat)

Aloha Shifters - Jewels of the Heart

Lure of the Dragon (Book 1)

Lure of the Wolf (Book 2)

Lure of the Bear (Book 3)

Lure of the Tiger (Book 4)

Love of the Dragon (Book 5)

Lure of the Fox (Book 6)

Aloha Shifters - Pearls of Desire

Rebel Dragon (Book 1)

Rebel Bear (Book 2)

Rebel Lion (Book 3)

Rebel Wolf (Book 4)

Rebel Heart (A prequel to Book 5)

Rebel Alpha (Book 5)

Fire Maidens - Billionaires & Bodyguards

Fire Maidens: Paris (Book 1)

Fire Maidens: London (Book 2)

Fire Maidens: Rome (Book 3)

Fire Maidens: Portugal (Book 4)

Fire Maidens: Ireland (Book 5)

The Wolves of Twin Moon Ranch

Desert Hunt (the Prequel)

Desert Moon (Book 1)

Desert Blood (Book 2)

Desert Fate (Book 3)

Desert Heart (Book 4)

Desert Rose (Book 5)

Desert Roots (Book 6)

Desert Yule (a short story)

Desert Wolf: Complete Collection (Four short stories)

Sasquatch Surprise (a Twin Moon spin-off story)

Shifters in Vegas

Paranormal romance with a zany twist

Gambling on Trouble

Gambling on Her Dragon

Gambling on Her Bear

Serendipity Adventure Romance

Off the Charts

Uncharted

Entangled

Windswept

Adrift

Travel Romance

Veiled Fantasies

Island Fantasies

visit www.annalowebooks.com

About the Author

USA Today and Amazon bestselling author Anna Lowe loves putting the "hero" back into heroine and letting location ignite a passionate romance. She likes a heroine who is independent, intelligent, and imperfect – a woman who is doing just fine on her own. But give the heroine a good man – not to mention a chance to overcome her own inhibitions – and she'll never turn down the chance for adventure, nor shy away from danger.

Anna loves dogs, sports, and travel – and letting those inspire her fiction. On any given weekend, you might find her hiking in the mountains or hunched over her laptop, working on her latest story. Either way, the day will end with a chunk of dark chocolate and a good read.

Visit AnnaLoweBooks.com

Printed in Great Britain
by Amazon